ADRIFT IN TIME

Roberto Pazzi

ADRIFT IN TIME

Translated from the Italian
by Vivien Sinott

ANDRE DEUTSCH

First published in Great Britain in 1991 by
André Deutsch Ltd
105–106 Great Russell Street, London WC1B 3LJ

Translation Copyright © 1991 by Vivien Sinott

Originally published in Italian as *La Malattia del Tempo*
by Marietti, Genoa, in 1987
Copyright © 1987 by Garzanti Editore s.p.a., Milan

British Library Cataloguing in Publication Data
Pazzi, Roberto, *1946–*
    Adrift in time.
    I. Title
    853–914 [F]

    ISBN 0 233 98715 0

Printed in Great Britain by
Billings and Son, Worcester

ADRIFT IN TIME

═══ Prelude ═══

"THE WORLD will tremble at her reawakening, Gourgaud. Let China sleep; leave her dozing. . ." So saying the grand exile of St. Helena pulled at the bridle of his mount to avoid a rocky outcrop on the narrow path leading from the western flank of Diana's Peak to his Longwood residence. Evening had fallen, and the view over the ocean changed and changed again under the fading rays of the setting sun. So had come the end of another long monotonous day, distinguished only from others preceding it when marked off on the calendar by a stroke of General Gourgaud's pen, this being his appointed task. It had been the sudden appearance of a wagon loaded with casks of brandy that had brought the Emperor and his retinue to a halt even though the two Chinese drivers had checked the pace of their yoked oxen. The inhabitants of St. Helena included a colony of Chinese whose lot, for the last hundred and fifty years, had been to serve the English, lords of the island, in all the most menial tasks. Seeing the Emperor so thoughtful, staring fixedly at the two little men on top of the cart, neither Gourgaud nor Montholon spoke but merely motioned the drivers to move on and leave the path free.

The Emperor's remark about the reawakening of China had puzzled them and they felt disinclined for any further talk that might disturb their lord's train of thought. Even later, when the Chinese and their wagon had disappeared, the slow and cautious pace at which he rode made them feel that comment or conversation would be unwelcome. For several days past his moods had alternated between excitement and long hours of silence as if his mind were constantly filled by a single idea, as if his too inactive body were more than ever vibrating at the vision conjured up by this idea. It had all begun on September 5th 1817 when Dr. Barry E. O'Meara, examining the Emperor in his bedchamber, had shown him that strange little volume which had just arrived on the ship bringing mail and books from England. It was entitled "Manuscript mysteriously received from St. Helena", authorship being attributed to the Emperor himself. A note by the publisher John Murray, however, expressed doubts on this point suggesting that it might have been written by Benjamin Constant or Madame de Staël. Lord Bathurst, Secretary of State for the Colonies, had evidently sent it out to the exile not only as an act of courtesy but also to observe his reactions.

Gourgaud, Montholon and the other Frenchmen in the prisoner's entourage had seen how their lord became immersed in that strange imaginary autobiography, never stopping until he had finished it. So impetuous was his every gesture that they, aided by the Countess de Montholon, had been obliged to take turns at noting all the Emperor's comments on the many errors the book contained, as well as the things which he acknowledged he might well have said or thought. However once having finished the work of commenting on and glossing over that 'actor's script', written for him to recite – which so disturbingly relegated him and his life to the portrait gallery of history in advance of time – the Emperor had relapsed into his former state of boredom and stupor, roused only when something from those pages seemed suddenly to flash across his mind. The ghost of his life was travelling far from St. Helena like a creature already independent and mature, able to reply for him, to affirm, lie, specify, reveal, hide, mock or be ironic in his place. A ghost, gradually sucking from him what life he still retained, seemed to be living in his stead, rushing from one court to another, from one ministry to another, from one capital to another of the Europe once his own, his prize of war, defeated and subdued, but now showing indifference to the theft, by that ghostly shadow, of his very existence while all the time his real self was confined on a rock in the Atlantic. As a result of reading about that false self of his, a self so like him in certain moods, he had come to believe for the first time in a truth even more terrible than the death he knew could not be long delayed on so unhealthy and inhospitable an island; he, who had outlived his times and personal freedom, would have to endure, in advance, a process deforming his own existence, like any captive that history delivers over to that most ruthless of prison warders, time itself.

Because, rather than life, this was mere survival from a past age – as if through a crack in his prison cell he had seen what the dead manage to avoid knowing and seeing. One night, unperceived by his most faithful intimates – whom he felt he hated as warders, different from the English but no less final – he had made a vain attempt to write down the history of his life, even though he knew he had no literary gifts, as a bare chronicle of facts.

Even Caesar had succeeded, and had not their lives been somewhat similar? Had not he also ruled the world for twenty years? Certainly, in cutting him down at the height of his power death had been kind to Caesar, a kindness denied to himself; both had nevertheless been able to conquer the world just as if they had both been called upon to repeat a single plan conceived by a superior mind which, in its unlimited inventiveness, could appreciate the subtle, ironic, unavoidable temptation of constant repetition. For a few hours he had written feverishly, unaware of how long he had spent in filling up so many sheets with his large angular handwriting full of flourishes and angry crossings out. It was he who was alive, real and authentic; he who could still return to Europe, control his own destiny, grasp the hands of the clock, turn them fast once more, win again as he had always won. Why, he was not yet even fifty. . . That other one, usurping the truth as he himself knew it in Europe, that false Emperor in the book passing through the hands of millions of people, greedily read about by so many who loved and hated him – he would defeat this usurper, silence him, show what he himself really was, what he really had done, decided, hidden, pretended to be, he would show who were those he had loved, who were those he had overcome. . . And as his writing covered more and more of the paper he became possessed by a fierce joy that had not been his since the days of the battlefields.

Dawn came and, with it, cold awareness. As soon as the first milky light of a new day of captivity on St. Helena began to filter through the closed shutters, remembrance of the present burst over his head like an avalanche. He could hear Marchand, his faithful servant, beginning to move about, lighting the fire and getting his lord's bath ready; he could make out the picture of his little heir and young Austrian wife on the mantelpiece near the mirror. He gazed round him like a drunken man, recognised the dreary room, the ceiling which still smelled of the paint and pitch used for repairs made since the monsoon. He looked down at his ink-stained hands, at his nightgown half open revealing his growing paunch; he even seemed to taste a shade of the unpleasant breath which had been worrying his doctor for some time past. What could he have been doing? What were all those sheets under his hand? Had he been dreaming? Had he started to write his memoirs? How could he have allowed himself to think of such a thing, even for an instant? All the events of his reign were well enough known and it was not for him to pander to public curiosity. But what had he thought he was doing? Competing with some arrogant hack who had copied his style and had drawn inspiration from the greatness of his deeds? No, nobody could ever distort one moment of his life or one single action; neither could he ever fall so low as to dispute the truth, his truth, with anyone. For him silence was best, only so could it maintain at its full stature the legendary figure he had created. In this manner was his glorification beginning; the phantom that threatened him in Europe, that had written his life for him, would soon be overtaken by imitators – not one or two, not three but a hundred, a thousand would appear writing in as many languages, all claiming to be the true autobiographer. Before long legions of historians and poets would gain possession of a letter, of a story, of some piece of evidence, of a tale told by some fellow soldier. Why had he so feared the sight of that first sign of worship for the legend he was about to become, now that martyrdom was putting the touch of perfection on his existence?

Writing his own life would have been as cowardly as flight from St. Helena. To keep silent and waste away on that island was just as great an achievement as was action and fighting all over Europe and in Egypt. He must take away with him the secret of his making, the seal of what he really was, he must remain a mystery. Woe betide him if he yielded to any desire to explain his deeds and thoughts; his fate would be as miserable as that of writers and artists who enviously simulate the power of the great men of history. St. Helena must be his tomb, his mausoleum, his brightest halo, brighter perhaps than that of Austerlitz.

With that he picked up the sheets and began tearing them up until they were a heap of tiny pieces, buttoned his nightshirt and put on his dressing gown. Closing the inkwell he moved it well away, and replied to his servant Marchand as calmly as he did every morning. In the next room the fire was burning and into the flames he threw that impossible autobiography, poking with the tongs to make sure every bit was burnt and that no fragment of the truth remained.

That was the day, September 5th 1817, when, riding home towards evening, he had met the Chinese and had made the remark which the two courtiers had let pass without comment. General Gourgaud believed it must relate in some way to the false Emperor's manuscript and decided he would read it again to see if it did contain any mention of China. Montholon, on the other hand, more alert and sensitive to the Emperor's state of mind, decided that henceforward he would check the mail and newspapers arriving from Europe even if it meant hiding from his lord anything he thought might be upsetting. For that matter the entire entourage, twenty in all, felt the problem of his changeable temper. Should it be necessary to keep something back from him in order to preserve a serene atmosphere among them all, he would accept responsibility for doing so. He pondered for a while over that comment about China. But who could help them from the East? What had the Emperor meant when he said that one day the world would tremble when that great nation reawoke?

FIRST
MOVEMENT

1

THE TARTAR cavalry fringed the high banks of the Po. The long march from Mongolia and from China, across lands little known but famous for their ancient civilizations, had come to an end. One by one frontiers had given way, collapsed like a house of cards; Russia first, immense and heroic with her millions of dead, then the Balkan countries, pale shadows of Russia, then Germany, within the space of a day returning to the desolate plains that appeared as they had to Germanicus' Roman Legions two thousand years before.

Aiku himself had said that no one could stop them, neither the Russians with their terrible weapons, nor the allied forces from over the ocean who were unwilling to move a single soldier, content to remain undisturbed in control of their continent. The sophisticated weapons he had wrested from the Russians – atomic bombs and missiles handled, at his orders, by an army of experts and scientists – had achieved his objective. He himself felt a strong aversion for those diabolical machines and, to avoid losing the position of command that came so naturally to him, had forbidden his twelve generals to learn their use. Thus had it been written:

only a river flowing over a wide plain beyond the highest mountains in Europe would contain their victorious advance. Farther than that they must not go; but nothing of this was to be said to the crowds behind the standard bearing the white nine-tailed yak that Aiku had brought with him in a revival of ancient Tartar unity. Now it would be no easy matter to hold in check the destructive fury, the impetuous drive of the hordes who, though he could not speak their tongues, obeyed him as leader as if they had always recognised the language of victory. Would they now accept a truce, would they obey an order to stop on the banks of a river, certainly a big one but nothing to compare with the lake-wide rivers they had crossed in Siberia? And from there over the Urals as far as the shorter though no less majestic rivers of the German plains? Yet some exceptional decision must have entered their minds right from the first light of dawn when a million men, ranked in thousands upon thousands on the left bank of the Po, had begun to discern the square towers of a city, with its churches and mansions, through the bluish haze lying over the plain.

What could be hidden in that hollow? A logical question because the ancient city seemed to be sinking into a depression in the plain, as if time had eroded its foundations preparing its return to the earth, half-decayed, already surrendering. Only towers and campanili seemed to indicate the presence of houses as yet invisible. Accompanied by the twelve officers of his high command, Aiku anxiously rode back and forth along the Veneto side of the river, where the sight of two bridges, one destroyed the other still usable, seemed to suggest alternative destinies for the city, irreconcilable but none the less urgent to him who was putting it under threat. To cross over, as the glances of so many pressed him to do? Or to camp where they stood, bring the invasion to an end, begin setting to rights an empire covering half the world?

Aiku borrowed binoculars from Ethelbert, his German second-in-command, a man who, thrown out by his government, had promptly revealed so many of his country's secrets. To Aiku there was something familiar about that city of the plain . . . Omsk, Lvov, Vilnius. But no, none of those, no city in Siberia, Ukraine, Poland, Brandenburg possessed that same azure tranquillity . . . Though sunk into the vast bed of the plain, it looked warlike with its geometrical towers, so square and moulded. The Kremlin towers, many more and much taller, seemed like the sisters of the churches, imploring protection from Heaven. These however did no such thing; they looked capable of withstanding long sieges as perhaps many times they had done centuries earlier, an impression strengthened by that one piece of wall showing above the hollow in which the city was sunk. Looking to the right and left Aiku tried to recall its name, barely heard from the officer on guard, the night after Venice and Padua had capitulated to one of the Mongolian units. He was still uncertain whether it was that soldier who had uttered the name, so sleepy had he been the night the first reconnaissance group returned from the Po: Ferrara . . .

All that could be seen in the plain on either side were a few houses, some peaceful farms, and long rows of fruit trees. Now and again shrilling cicadas drowned the murmur of the hive of soldiers fringing the banks. The road to the one serviceable bridge led to the hollow that hid the city, no doubt about that. Seen through binoculars it was wide, inviting and well kept, with plane trees and large stones placed at regular intervals along its sides. Only a few lorries and cars bore witness to the flight of the last fugitives towards the city; possibly seeking safety, though their composed, almost unhurried movement seemed to deny any such belief. At Padua, when the first houses were sighted, the spectacle had been much more traditional; his advance had been accompanied by the usual appeals to the generosity of the conqueror.

There in that rich and populous city, proudly arrogant in the centuries-old protection of its saint, who when alive had so often censured its cowardice, the appeals had become offers of hidden gold and jewels, attempts at seduction by beautiful women sent to implore his pity – such unseemliness arousing in Aiku a dislike much greater than if their husbands had stoutly resisted his attack.

In his tent he had given them all the satisfaction they sought – uttering no word, using no language save that of bodies locked in struggle but lacking that subtle taste of adventure and death which had lured him to invade their land. As for these ornaments of Padua who passed their days beside their corrupt and high-ranking husbands – concerned only with showing off their positions of privilege – he ignored the pleas of these beauties, consigning them to his officers whose pleasure therefore took second place to that of their leader; so that, like the rich German ladies and the wives of Russian potentates, these women might also experience the long-dreamed but never avowed emotion of rape.

Nothing of the kind, however, had marked his advance towards the city that now lay before him, though still partly hidden from his gaze by the slight depression in the alluvial plain.

No one had come out to beg mercy, to attempt negotiation, as if the city were defended by sleep or indifference. This fatalism also had struck him as a further sign that the river before him formed an impassable barrier, perhaps the very one he had known he would meet since he left his own land in the Yablonovy mountains north of China.

His train of thought was interrupted by the shouts of some soldiers not far from the point where he had left the sappers

14

and engineers trying to raise the broken section of the fallen bridge.

"General, those soldiers want to wade the river on horseback at once. We have been hard put to it to stop them . . ." shouted one of Ethelbert's adjutants.

So now he would have to issue a clear order, end his indecision, settle all doubts.

"What news from France?" With sudden inspiration Aiku turned abruptly to the leader of the Koreans.

"Paris has fallen, the Government resigned yesterday evening. We expect to control the whole country within twenty-four hours. Our forces are performing miracles."

Miracles, he thought, just the miracle I could work here, on this peaceful sunlit plain, among these fruit trees with the cicadas, in these wheatfields, among those towers yonder. A single order, just one, after that nothing could be as before. An order is like a minute in time, irrevocable. Instead, a certain day of his childhood suddenly came to mind when his grandfather's complaining voice kept calling him back into the house on seeing him at play in the dusty streets of Urga.

"Aiku, come here . . . I have something to tell you. Come in . . ." Only rarely did his grandfather call him by name; he was nearing death, suffering from the same disease from which all the male members of Aiku's family slowly died. They began by refusing food and gradually lost their sight, confusing the dead with the living, telling stories of seventy or eighty years before, gazing round with greater intensity than they had done when they could see, as if, at last, their now sightless eyes were able to perceive things around them in that sparsely inhabited country where one could walk for days without meeting a fellow creature. Aiku's eyes also had possessed that strange familiarity with stones, sand and mountain cliffs which in Mongolia slowly inured the old to

15

avoid contact with the living. That day his grandfather had taken hold of his left hand – Aiku had never forgotten the shudder than ran through him at the trembling senility of the old man's touch – passing across it the wrinkled palm of his other as if searching in that childish hand signs foretelling the future, a future of stars and travel covering a span of life. Still holding Aiku's hand he had whispered with rising agitation these incomprehensible words, "Aiku, you will stop at a river, when the city sinks before you. Remember that . . . I too now would continue but no, my time is over."

Only then, so many years later, on the banks of the Po with the city sunk in its hollow before him, did he understand those words spoken by his grandfather shortly before he died. And he must obey them though such wandering talk would be useless as an explanation for his decision to stop the advance. Power and solitude went hand in hand; high time he learned that, so why hesitate? Shading his eyes from the sun, Aiku searched once more to right and left for someone who would dissuade him from what he had to do, some force, some form like his own, a dream within his dream, a god . . . But over there things were just as they had been, just as before . . . Nothing now to delay his decision so, handing the binoculars back to Ethelbert, he called over the other traitor, the Georgian Poliakoff who, on losing his seat on the Politbureau, had at once gone over to the enemy.

"Poliakoff, call a general halt! At long last we have arrived."

He knew well how that crooked one-eyed character possessed the rare gift of making himself understood in no less than seventeen languages. There were more than that spoken in his army but the Russian could always manage and, on occasion, the radio and other sophisticated instruments he had taught them to use in Russia and Germany spread the voice of Aiku to all corners of the earth. Most of the Tartars, especially those who had left Urga with him, but even more the throngs of men who had joined his ranks from Outer Mongolia and from China, now showed reluctance to obey the order. The prevailing atmosphere was one of willingness to halt for the present; to pause but not to stop. In the vast camps, in the houses requisitioned along the Po, where the most important logistic bases had been set up for hundreds of miles down to the delta, the ferment among the troops, brought to a halt after advancing for two years, was as potent and awe-inspiring as the march itself; an immense ants' nest of souls unable to divine the real intentions of their god. For Aiku, who had freed them from freedom, who had offered them all a destiny, must surely have a plan in mind. He was merely gaining time. It was unthinkable that a river should hold him back, that a warrior of his stature should be intimidated by the sight of that city sunk in its haze of heat. They must surely be going to advance beyond it.

"But as far as where? We shall have to stop somewhere, shan't we? When we can see no more land to conquer, where shall we go?"

"When there is nothing in front of us we shall make an about turn and everything will seem as it was before, you'll see! Someone will have rebelled, we shall have to go back and give them a lesson – maybe in Russia where they are tougher. Ah, were it only possible once more to cross those plains in summer, once again to sleep in a square in Kharkov, sense the fear, admiration, amazement in the women's eyes . . .". Thus two Chinese, who had been gazing across the river as if seeing some magical elusive country, tried to repress their suspicions that perhaps Aiku really had decided not to cross it. The elder of the two had hidden in his haversack a gilded statuette of Saint Gertrude, stolen from a church in Lublin during the invasion of Poland and, unable to pray and confess his fears to nothing, and, having no sacred image from home, had lately, hiding the fact from his fellow soldiers, been confiding his secret wishes to that image of a saint so nearly resembling a child. It seemed too that this female divinity had begun to smile at him, especially since he had promised to take her back to her convent in Lublin should his desire of returning to Kharkov ever be fulfilled; in a few months time, in that battered city, Irina, the Ukranian girl he had loved during the army's long stay there, would bear him a son. That month the Mongolian armies had been ordered to move into southern Russia, Ukraine and the Crimea so as to complete occupation of the country which had endeavoured on Europe's behalf to stem the advance of those terrible hordes who had defied all efforts of international diplomacy to restore peace. No western authority, neither the Secretary of the United Nations, nor the American President, the King of England, nor the Pope had found a way of dealing with Aiku's fury of devastation, Aiku the Mongol, the man who had promised to lead his despised people to world domination.

So it had been that, after desperate Russian resistance along the Don and the Dnieper, his army had broken through their lines and had occupied the whole country. No surviving Russian hated Aiku as he hated that traitor who, after in-doctrinating his countrymen for forty years, had brought about their ruin by taking sides with the invader when excluded from succession to the last dictator.

Irina, realising she was pregnant, had said the same thing one night to her Chinese lover. "I do not hate your people even though I curse your Aiku. No, though I don't hate you, I would give my life to kill Poliakoff."

"But now you must live, Irina. You must think of our child. I shall come back and we shall go and live together somewhere, it matters little whether here or in China, or over there in Europe. The world is a big place and we can make a home anywhere."

"Yes, for you it is like that. Aiku has neither home nor country. It is all his now."

Many of the Tartar soldiers, without a country but at home wherever they won, felt the same as the Russian girl in Kharkov. Home was farther on, towards the plain or the mountain, over the lake or the river, on the other side of that range, that stretch of sea; everything beyond that was home. Not all of them who knew they had generated children of a new race during that invasion – taking to themselves the women of their defeated foes – longed for a home as did the Chinese from Canton who prayed to the gilded statuette stolen in Lublin. Most of them did not care to see the children born from that churning up of peoples and races. It was as if the huge stream of men sweeping over Europe like an immense tidal wave was to create a new world scene, a new humanity.

Having arrested the Government, taken over the nation's power stations, military bases and strong points, and having sunk nearly the whole fleet, Aiku's words, spoken at the Grand Council of Tartars in the hall of Catherine II at the Kremlin in Moscow, had been of startling clarity. "May a new world arise from the blood to be shed! The time has come for humanity to be reborn and to replace the old. Nothing can save Europe, her gods are in flight."

On this point there had been much lively discussion among council members. Aiku's first and most faithful followers did not all agree; with him they had gained the Yablonovy mountains for the guerillas, fought back the Russian invader and freed Mongolia. Ude was to remain behind to govern Russia while the main army was being reorganised in Europe;

19

he wanted the Tartar forces – Mongols, Chinese, Koreans, Samoyeds and Manchurians – to join with the Russians in ruling their country thus forming an amalgam of peoples; Subotai, however, who was to return to the east to govern there in Aiku's absence, sternly opposed any such plan.

"How can you think that our people would agree to work, on a basis of parity, alongside those they have defeated? Did we go to war just for that? Aiku, your men found courage to follow you because they admired your victories, not because of your clemency. You cannot stop now! The Tartars would become disunited once again, divided, subdued."

And so Aiku had delayed his supreme decision, whether to govern a people surviving as serfs or become one of them; he knew that one day he would have to stop at a river bank. But in his own mind his decision was already made: a new race was to arise from his war, a race able to combine the highest qualities of west and east, of the conquered and the conquerors. The world would owe him gratitude, him the Mongol from an obscure village where the impure feet of the foreigner had never trodden, where only the legend that far beyond the enclosing circle of mountains there was another world and another people with white skins had coloured his childish dreams and play; until that time when his grandfather has spoken those strange words about a river he would be unable to cross; and that city which nothing could save from sinking, that, also evoked by his grandfather in delirium, had aroused a lightning image of tall houses, bridges, towers and mansions. In spite of this, though still undecided how to treat these conquered peoples or what policy to adopt in those hitherto independent countries, added one at a time to his new empire, Aiku felt a sudden surge of rage and had reacted sharply when told that one of his lieutenants left behind in Poland, seduced by a beautiful Catholic, had become entangled in the eternal fray between communists and believers and, in a single night in Warsaw, had allowed over two thousand militant communist party members to be put to death.

"I have no intention of conquering the world just to create a replica of it. Hang that wretch and his girl", had been his order.

That evening, the first of the truce after the order to halt had been given, he had climbed the banks of the Po, in the dying twilight, for another look at the hollow in the plain into which the square towers of the city seemed to sink. While his horse impatiently pawed the ground, Aiku once more raised the binoculars to view from afar what he would never see close to. Now, master of half the world and feared throughout the whole of it, facing the lights of that city twinkling in the dark, he felt exiled and powerless in a way for which no victory won during the last two years could compensate.

Doubts assailed him of having misunderstood what he was meant to do, of having dreamed the words of his grandfather and those of other men impelled by prophetic insight. From them, at different times, places, circumstances and occasions – in a Lhasa convent, on Tamerlane's tomb in Samarkand, at the Mecca, in a Rangoon temple, before the shaman at Urga – had always come the same warning:

"Stop at the river where a sunken city will lie before you."

2

RIGHT FROM his waking moments it had been a horrible day. The Holy Father had risen earlier than usual, troubled by a dream which seemed to diffuse a leaden atmosphere over events following hard one upon another.

In his dream he had lost himself in a ravine among the high mountains of a country unknown to him, along whose eastward peaks ran a curving embattlement wall similar to the Great Wall of China. After travelling the valley road for an immeasurable time he could perceive in the fading light a town built up the side of the valley. He could make out the poorer single-storey dwellings near a narrow stream; higher up were the mansions of the richer class, temples and towers rising towards a large severe-looking building whose windowless steel walls, bright as mirrors, still reflected the last light of the sun. The town was entirely deserted but appeared as if only just abandoned by its inhabitants. A great pot still bubbled on a fire inside a house, the door flung wide. A garment or two hanging on pegs seemed still to retain the shape of the body that had worn them a few minutes earlier. Doors stood open, carts fully loaded had been left untended in the streets, a light breeze played over everything, moving curtains and shutters, blowing leaves. He walked on, seeking whomever there must surely be in that town still breathing vitality, on until, after a tiring climb, his white robes grey with dust, he reached the steely-walled building and found himself facing a single door fully opened. From the great entrance hall a light shone. He went in. Among the thousand lighted candles he recognised, lying on a catafalque, his own corpse, clothed in snow white robes, his mitre on his head and, on his feet, red velvet shoes with gold buckles.

Throughout the whole of that terrible day, while more and more disturbing news continued to arrive, his thoughts had often returned to his dream. That evening he had gone to bed very late. There had been a long discussion of events with his closest collaborators after agitated telephone conversations with the American President, the Secretary of the United Nations, the President of France who had fled to Corsica from Paris, and with the Italian government. What to do now with 'him' at the gates? Let him advance, await him at the City or sally forth to meet him, speak with him, try every means of negotiation? Total disagreement prevailed among the great powers. Some urged him to stay in Rome, others besought him to go and parley with Aiku personally. Throughout Italy, while radio and television gave out the latest news, more dissatisfaction was felt in people's homes with the government than with this cursed 'Scourge of God'; the government had appeared wavering, hesitant, disunited, incapable of taking anything approaching a decision. The only thing known was that an armoured division had been sent north.

"But which way did they send them?" the Pope had asked his secretary.

"Towards the Po, your Holiness."

"And now", added Monsignor Della Genga, a prelate who boasted among his ancestors one of the most reactionary of all the popes, "Aiku can take a good look at the river from where he is."

Later, in the depths of night, when at last his collaborators had retired and when it seemed clear that all the western leaders had lost their heads, the Pope felt he could no longer seek advice from any of those faint-hearts nor attempt the useless task of giving it. Only God's counsel could help him. All at once he felt an urge to go and pray in the Sistine chapel in which, years before, one mild spring morning, he had risen from his cell to hear himself proclaimed successor to Peter. Accompanied by only a prelate along an intricate series of corridors, across inner courtyards, up stairways and in lifts, he had reached the chapel so beautified by the work of Michelangelo. Passing a moment before through the Clementine chapel, where one day he would lie in state like so many of his predecessors, he had paused in wonder as if not even the total certainty of the ceremony attending his own death could assure him of his presence among the living. Death too was subject to a new variable. Motioning the prelate to leave him, he had knelt to pray in the light of two candles on the altar. Dense was that vast obscurity, dense as had been the passage of time since, clothed in white, they had escorted him to the central balcony of St. Peter's. The trembling candlelight scarcely penetrated the emptiness up to the vault, illuminating the blessed and the damned on the Day of Judgement; he could barely recall the features of his younger self, the motions of that extraordinary hour, his first words, the faces around him.

Once again the cardinals had chosen a man from the east. To them it seemed that a Lithuanian like himself could maintain the tradition set by his predecessor, since support by the Slav world could aid the Church in bringing Christianity to peoples of antique faith and healthy morals, less afflicted than those in the west by the blight of affluence. The 'beloved Italian nation' had given to the Church popes of an accommodating nature, hesitant over denouncing the evils of their society, fearful of opening the great Book of Revelations of St. John the Divine and of reading the signs of the times therein. His predecessor, that venerable and charismatic figure, had called him to his side in the Curia in the latter years of his pontificate; and towards the end, when illness prevented his worldwide travels, had promoted him cardinal and more and more frequently had urged the members of the Holy See to give him preferment, adopting a style more in line with the ways and customs of a hereditary dynasty than those of a dignity to which they were elected by the Holy Spirit. But their last meeting at the old Pope's deathbed had been dramatic; thrombosis had impaired his speech and his pupil could barely comprehend the significance of the dying man's words uttered between gasps for breath. Yet he felt certain he had understood those terrible words; now, on that evening, kneeling at the feet of the Christ portrayed in the Day of Judgement, they came back to him, graver, more applicable today than ever before. It was those words which, just as they were proclaiming him Pope, had taken him back a month earlier to the dying man's bedside and had distracted for an instant his attention from the question put him by the cardinal; what name, as Peter's successor, had he chosen?

"You will be the one . . . to meet him . . . you will go . . . the Antichrist too comes from the East . . . stop him . . . you will know him . . .".

And while replying "Leo" to the cardinal's question, his thoughts returned to Attila and the 'Scourge of God'.

For years now he had been wondering what destiny those prophetic words of that dearly loved man had tried to

25

announce. He well knew that he owed his election to him, ever since the day the Pope had summoned him to Rome from the episcopal seminary of Saint Casimir in Vilnius, impressed as he was by the primate's report informing him that the most forceful teacher in the seminary was this son of a Baltic fisherman. Years later when on a journey to Canada, having succeeded the old man as guide of the Church, he had been asked by an Armenian journalist what he thought of the Mongol Aiku. Aiku by then was invading eastern Siberia, had roused the Mongolians against the Russians, allied them with the Chinese, and was now intending to conquer the sickly nations of Europe. To this question he had felt unable to reply as if hoping to banish the threat by ignoring it. The world seemed already so poisoned with false prophets, with bloodthirsty political leaders . . . This one would also drown in the same blood he caused to flow. Since then, however, he had never been able to elude the question. On his return journey to Rome he had already heard more news of that man – disconcerting, atrocious, some even incredible. At Lisbon airport, receiving homage from the President, he had wondered for the first time, without even himself realising why, if that madman would reach so far, if indeed the Atlantic itself would stop him. So regretful was he of this momentary distraction, and of the consequent confused reply he gave to the President's words, that he did not wish to mention the matter again, not even to his Secretary at the Nuncio's residence later on.

Nevertheless he had been obliged to return to it when woken in the middle of the night by Monsignor Della Genga who was overcome with fright: "Your Holiness, he has taken Moscow and is advancing towards Poland . . ." Still sleepy, he had thought of that other warrior who had taken Moscow but had not come from the East. What meaning lay behind this reversal of direction? Suddenly he recalled the words of his predecessor: "the Antichrist will come from the east . . ." From that night on he had constantly thought about the man. Who was Aiku? Where did he come from? What reason prompted his action? Had he some plan or was he moved merely by a blind impulse to conquer like Genghis Khan and Tamberlane? But no situation in all history was comparable to this. The arms he possessed were too terrible and sophisticated; he had managed to capture Russian weapons, and nearly a billion Asians obeyed his orders as if following some god. He had announced, rumour said, that if even half that number died, with the remaining five hundred million he could conquer the world.

His actions had already caused untold millions of victims by using only a few times those terrible weapons that had drained Russia's resources dry, and which – by some strange chance of fate – had been turned against the Russians themselves. In him there seemed to be a strange mixture of the ascetic and the sensual, of the Mephistophelian and the simple, always travelling with a squadron of horsemen though he could well have made use of any modern means. Along his road he consulted seers and soothsayers, prayed to every god in the lands he conquered, accepting none yet venerating all. His followers included a multitude of astrologers, magicians, charlatans, holy men, hermits, gurus, and an incalculable number of concubines often torn, during his advance, from their families and villages, from the highly placed, even from potentates. Inexplicably he surrounded himself with traitors whom it pleased him to confer honours upon and to appoint to crucial positions: his intimates included a German and a Russian, Ethelbert and the crafty Poliakoff, two political figures who for years had handled affairs in their own countries and knew them better than anyone. It was even rumoured that in every country his able agents had set up such close networks of secret allies and spies as to make it increasingly likely that other heads of state would soon follow the example of that cynical Bulgarian who, with his whole government, had passed over to the Mongol's side, declaring by radio that resistance was useless, surrender advisable; if other countries decided to follow his wise example, he said, Europe, torn and divided for centuries, would become united.

What could be done against such a man? The Pope, alone and unprepared, appeared faced with this awful historical responsibility. No one in that hour could help him!

Europe expected from him some gesture, some message, some decision. Her governments had by now become resigned to the worst as if mesmerised by some fatal force. That demon had not won by human reasoning; he possessed a charisma more potent than weapons.

Why had it not been his lot to steer the boat of St. Peter in another age? Calm and peaceful pontificates there had been, lasting twenty-seven days, a year, a few months, passing like the wind over a troubled but still human world, sick but still vital. What was happening now, however, went far beyond the range of history. And it had happened to him, not to his proud and combative predecessor; to him, so weak at heart, outwardly so decisive but inwardly in such torment . . . In this chapel, for five hundred years the Holy Spirit had descended to enlighten, with the principles of the Church, minds assembled from all parts of the world. For a moment he imagined he saw them gathered there in the gloom – fifty or so successors of Peter down the centuries. Silent, severe, frowning, as if weighing up his moral strength, his faith, his heroism. Yes, enough of words, enough of magnificent sermons from the balcony of St. Peter's, from under Bernini's canopy, beneath the dome . . . It is time for deeds, for courage in the hour of death, they seemed to whisper.

One in particular he distinguished more clearly, a tall, slight figure whose thin white beard framed his long brown face, one who stood out from the rest and made as if to step forward. Barnabas Chiaramonti, Pius VII: he who, for fifteen years, had withstood another terrible despot twice come to imprison him and take him far from Rome. Some historians had branded that saintly man as weak and feeble-minded. "He would have made a good parish priest but never a Pope of Rome," Metternich had once said of Pius VII. Stopping for the night at Radicofani on his way to exile, what remorse Pius – a defenceless prisoner – must have felt on thinking how easily he had yielded? Perhaps the same as he himself was now experiencing since Aiku was already in Italy and he, as Pope, had made no decision to go and meet him. Because Leo XIV knew he must go. He had realised it in a flash on entering the Sistine chapel when his electric torch had lit up, first among the other figures sculptured by Michelangelo, that of the martyr Bartholomew, the apostle shown holding his own skin in his hand. The indomitable martyr who went as apostle to Armenia and had suffered the supreme outrage to bear witness in distant lands to faith in Christ. He too must go; his weakness was no reason for not doing so, neither was his physical fear. The saints had not found the courage needed to face danger before meeting it, they went forward dismayed with terror like other men. The miracle happened only later. Yes, he would have to go, and without delay. No politician could do what he could. Most likely the politicians were the ones to blame for such a rapid debâcle before the barbarous Mongol hordes: their shortsighted inability to see beyond party politics and the very advantages they derived from democracy had weakened the moral atmosphere. They

29

had become tainted by a mentality rife in that disastrous age when all that counted in state politics was the relative strength on each side, the force of numbers, of capital, of production. In the slothful passivity of succeeding centuries the Church, even its Head, had assumed the same habits and taken a part in the game. Thus the most vital element of his makeup had been sapped, stifling the energy he had drawn from his Lithuania, oppressed and persecuted even in her ethnic and spiritual identity; the Slav spirit ever capable of action in a state of heady irrationality. Perhaps it was this quality that urged the saints forward. And probably the devil himself had driven Aiku to leave his lonely village in the desert and lead the Tartar forces in his conquest of the world.

3

AIKU SEEMED restless, not entirely able to control a vague feeling of apprehension. Ethelbert was explaining the situation to the high command inside the large octagonal tent set up near the Po, the yurt on whose pole flew Aiku's standard bearing the white nine-tailed yak. Among his silent officers Ethelbert's monotonous nasal drone intoned peoples, races, capitals, plains, mountain ranges. But not for Aiku whose attention was fixed on the richly jewelled belt worn by Zeja sitting opposite him, on the stones shining in its buckle and on the handle of his dagger stuck in between belt and dress. Well did he know those red and black stones with golden streaks like cats' eyes. Years before they returned to graze their sheep, his grandfather and father had broken their backs hacking away at the veins in the mountains near Urga that concealed those precious stones. How varied were their names! Passing through Asia and Europe he had learned many of them but everywhere the sight of those jewels made the eyes of men and women shine with the same glint of desire, narrowed in a way reminiscent of a cat facing too bright a light. As a child he had longed to hurl all those stones down the well behind their house after he came to understand how they had invaded the lives of his father and grandfather, taking them far away each day to the mountains that yielded up its treasure, bringing them back at night – their faces drawn with a fatigue that only bed and sleep could ease. No time could be spared for him. Before that his father had spent whole evenings by his bedside recounting his adventures on Sakhalin; now he appeared consumed with weariness.

Sudden unnatural changes had come about at that time as if the discovery of those stones had been followed by an evil spell. Hordes of soldiers with fur caps and long fur coats had arrived in Mongolia from afar and, in no time at all, had obliged the local people to stay at home in the evening, to write their names on their doors and to try and remember that other name, the family name they all possessed even if unaware of it. Their grandfather, who about that time had lost his memory, recalling only the most absurd and unlikely events of seventy or eighty years before, had been roughly questioned by a soldier in the doorway almost broken in by his rifle butt; the old man really had not known the answer when asked about his name. Trying to recall what they could, his father and grandfather had found a syllable or two they could combine to form it. But the soldier seemed dissatisfied and, on leaving, had been so threatening that they felt bound to offer him one of those blood-red stones. Aiku, at any rate, had never learned that name hidden within his own. He had always connected it with a feeling of acute danger associated with the figure of the soldier holding his rifle butt against the door – a fear that, by saying it, another such spell as that conjured up by the soldiers would bring intruders to their house demanding their belongings, especially those stones. They must possess a magic power to change people, so red and shining were they, so bright and hard! He had seen them in brilliant necklaces on the beautiful women who had followed the soldiers from their homelands, travelling with them high up on their wagons, distant and unapproachable, whispering in a mysterious tongue that sounded fascinating on their lips. (The same tongue that, when spoken by those men, became as hard and hateful as violence itself: the Russian language.) When he asked his father why the soldiers wanted so much to know that other name and have it written on the door, the answer given him confirmed his fears. Generations of men and women had borne it all their lives, generations who had lived there, eaten, slept, had brought up children, seen their own physical decay gain ground daily, losing their memories like his grandfather, then dying. He had felt so afraid of that word that he had forgotten it at once.

They had always called him Aiku – only that – like those rare men who seemed of no descent, without fathers, born of themselves. His own father had given him this confidence, first alarming him but then adding that few men in the whole world were known by their first names; he had mentioned some, Genghis Khan, Tamberlane. Now here in the yurt with Ethelbert droning on, monotonously intoning a list of names of different parts of the earth, those cities, rivers, mountains, he glanced again at the red gems in Zeja's belt and, smiling, thought he had achieved his desire not to be confused with anyone who, before his time, might have breathed the same sound from a mouth now dead.

Only a shade of remorse for his father clouded that rare pleasure. Not towards his grandfather, more like himself in the divine delirium between reality and dreams that had accompanied him on the downward slope of his declining years. His father, he thought, had oppressed him, leaving him breathless, blinded by his peculiar strength, that force of the proper names vibrating in the rivers, in the seas, in the cities evoked by Ethelbert to explain their fresh plans for war and occupation. Listening to how his deputy associated him with the orders issued in his name, he was amazed to feel what strength became embodied in the mere breath, on the lips of a man, needed for pronouncing a name as short as 'Aiku' – equivalent, on his mother's island of Sakhalin, to the word 'man'. In his state of uncertain consciousness between reverie and memories, names seemed to rise and fall like the notes of a melody; Switzerland to be occupied, France to be governed, Berlin to clean up, Warsaw, Moscow, the Soviets, America protesting over the invasion of Switzerland, the President of the United States whose letter . . . And over all that confused cosmos of titles and names, one dominated – his own. Aiku had replied that . . ., Aiku desired that . . ., Aiku was aware that . . ., Aiku had decided that . . . .

How often had he noticed that, from the time he had become so greatly feared, no longer was anyone able to address him by his name . . . Perhaps only his old comrades, Ude and Zeja, had sometimes felt they could. One of the first, he now recalled, to make him conscious of that new solitude, had been his father, he who had rent the veil over his destiny, unsuspecting that one day his son would feel it as an act of oppression. When Aiku had assembled his companions in the mountains and, in increasingly audacious sorties, had created growing difficulties for the Russian occupation troops in Mongolia (chasing them out of the province of Urga and so becoming, within a few months, the national hero of that region of Asia), his father had taken little part in the explosion of Mongolian pride in her glorious son. As far as he could his father had avoided every opportunity of their meeting, always shrinking from any greater fame or celebration of that name, as if only in the silence and loneliness of his grazing flocks could he regain peace of mind.

Aiku had seen him less and less. In the little conversation between them, in his home-comings, acute unease prevented him from telling that silent man of his doings, his dreams, his victories, his grand plans all on the way to realisation. Only once had emotion overcome them both when, ever weaker and more infirm, his father had slipped off his chair unable to control his arthritic feet. Aiku had leaped forward to lift him up and lay him on his bed, the bed in which his father had slept alone for thirty years since the death of his wife, and where he himself as a child had listened to those long tales of adventure on Sakhalin. Holding his father in his arms he had felt his great weight, so heavy he could barely raise him; as if from their deep abyss all the past years carried by that form, once so young, light, handsome on the Japanese island where he had lived out his hour of love and happiness, now rose one by one pleading for a further span of life. But it was the odour of that old body which convinced him that nothing now could save his father and that, if he really loved him, he must respect his wish for silence, the modest desire to leave this world before the spectacle of his son's glory became unbearable to him. A sharp unpleasant smell of mould, hardly of flesh any longer, emanated from him as if to pursue a plan of self-destruction, to ward off help, like certain animals who repel the enemy with their stench. A few days later his father had disappeared without trace. They had come to tell him one evening at Urga when he was about to announce the advance that would take him across Asia and Europe to where he now was, in Italy, on the banks of the Po. They had said that none of his neighbours had seen him for three days; the last time was in a village several miles distant from Urga where a shepherd not much younger than he, had wondered at seeing Aiku's father so solitary and tired. Aiku had dismounted and gone to talk to the shepherd, anxious for any details he could

35

tell him. But he had given no order to search for his father. Better leave him to seek out a village where he could be just himself and not the father of Aiku, where no one would remind him that his name, that name alone, could not be mentioned. And while Ethelbert's voice broke in, bringing his attention back to headquarters, his thoughts returned to Mongolia, to the deserts and mountains as they must have appeared to the eyes of his father fleeing from life, to the endless stretches of sand and rocks in which were hidden the mines of black and red stones, once so precious, but now worked out, exhausted as was the will to live: that will to live infused into his father by violence, as in all human beings, in a spasm of pleasure of two bodies never tired of uniting into one. Let him be free to choose his death if he could not choose to live. Nature herself in the conquered countries seemed tired, terribly tired, shocked by the desire for repose of the human capacity for reason. Perhaps the crisis in social institutions had infected the seasons, the seas, mountains, deserts, animals. Spring and autumn had become little more than literary memories living in the paintings and works of art belonging to the past. In most of the world seasons of extreme cold were being followed by extreme heat, torrid, almost equatorial. News had just arrived from Berlin of rats as big as cats having begun to infest the half-destroyed city in some terrible rebellion against their natural state as keepers of darkness and night. They had had to mobilise squads of police to chase the rats back into the drains, once it was discovered that the central squares and streets were alive with them, obstructing the traffic in broad daylight. People were shocked to see how the cats fled from them, terrorised by beasts who from time immemorial had been objects of prey and plunder. Sinister news had also come from Leningrad. There it concerned the fish in the Baltic Sea and in the

Neva, swollen to the size of cetaceans; they were blocking
the port, the canals and the river till navigation had become
so dangerous that many ships had had to be used for catching
them instead of whales. The effects of atomic disturbance was
the icy comment by men of science.

But the most incredible news of all had come from the
Balkan peninsula. Just the day before, Aiku had heard about
a woman giving birth to seventeen babies at Constanta
in Romania, each weighing not more than three and a
half ounces. And those really Lilliputian creatures were
doing extremely well. Anthropologists were now saying
this possibility too should have been foreseen as new and
monstrous forms of the human race could be born with far-
reaching genetic mutations. So Aiku's thoughts turned again
to his dream of a new race, long nurtured in Mongolia where,
faced with the sight of his people, scattered and defenceless,
and defeated by a few regiments of Russian soldiers, he had
pondered insurrection and revenge, imagining that all those
stones dug up by his grandfather and father and all the other
shepherds perforce turned miners, by some miracle became
men, warriors, hordes of soldiers ready to invade Russia. So
vast was his country, so exposed to the forces of wind, snow
and rain, that it seemed as if only a divine race could one
day inhabit it entirely, as if its valleys, deserts, rocks, caravan
routes all rejected that over-weak and ephemeral race that
was humanity. He was recalled to reality by the map of
Europe that Ethelbert spread out in front of his chair on
the large table round which they were all seated, asking him
to express a decision. How crowded seemed those countries
now opening out before him! What a thick network there
was of lines, circles, hills and valleys, broad and narrow routes
in black and red. So many names that they were printed
one almost over another, hard to distinguish, names that

most likely had replaced earlier versions, like Vienna that somewhere he had lately read was once Vindobona. He had been right to put a king back in each of those ancient lands as, initially, he had decided to do only for Italy, Bulgaria, Romania, Greece, Albania and Croatia. It was easier to reach an understanding and issue orders where there was a single head of state. He remembered now that he must decide in which of those cities to call a conference of all his divisional chiefs and of the sovereigns restored to their thrones. That was the main purpose of this meeting, the mute expectation expressed by Ethelbert's silence. The first stage of his conquest was now over; a stable order must be established for that dominion which, it seemed, even Nature opposed by her monstrous state of derangement.

Without hesitation Aiku's right forefinger pointed to one name on the map of Europe: Vienna.

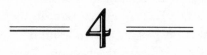

4

THE WATERLOO meeting had ended as Aiku wished. Guest of the King of Belgium in a castle on the plain of Waterloo, Aiku's thoughts reverted to his meeting the day before with the President of the United States of America – to his frenzied gestures, hurried handshakes, the ready mechanical smile on a face that immediately resumed its habitual mask-like appearance. Only a few years earlier Aiku had learned, as his troops slowly advanced across Siberia, that Europe lay beyond the Urals, that beyond Europe there was the ocean, that across the ocean was America – the powerful state governed by the man he had just met. Learning these things Aiku had known they would meet one day, though such a meeting was hard to imagine; as for the other heads of state, in Russia and in Europe, he had felt he knew them slightly before he actually met them. But that one? No, he seemed of a different mould, as if accustomed to commanding elements of time and space.

Now, waiting for Ethelbert and Poliakoff, he thought how easy it had been to divide the world into two zones of influence, the American zone all to the United States, with Europe, Asia and Africa, the old continent, to him. Easy, like splitting a ripe fruit, as if an invisible line already divided America and her President from the rest of the world. A line something like the one he had seen as a boy, on climbing one of the highest mountains in the Yablonovy range, when the shepherds had pointed out to him, in the blue distance, the Great Wall, a serpentine form outlining mountain after mountain, disappearing on the horizon. Beyond it, they told him, there had once been the Celestial Empire, and he had never forgotten the sight of the Wall losing itself among the mountains.

Everything had really gone so smoothly: the complaisant silence over the revolutions in Africa so as to allow him to assume control; creation of a power like Japan able to occupy the islands around Australia without taking either side, receptive to political control and to expansion of both their markets. There had been a moment, however, when Aiku had noted the expressive gaze of the American Secretary of State, a tall man of about fifty, white-haired, descendant of the astronomer whose name was linked to that of the comet, Edmund Halley.

Rather than hate for him personally, it seemed to Aiku that this gaze expressed incredulity, directed more towards the President than towards himself, as if some arrangement had now been made in total conflict with their prior understanding. Later when the Urga cavalry, parading triumphantly in their uniforms, as they had in so many world capitals, was galloping across the plain, Aiku suddenly noted once again the difference between the two Americans, so simulated had been the admiring attention of the President, so tense and pained that of the Secretary of State whose glance went from the riders to their chief and back again as if trying to solve a knotty problem, clear up some mystery. Aiku had felt he should show him respect, avoid tension, not speak directly to him.

40

With the President, however, he had chatted freely, exchanging quips as if to make up for his reserved attitude towards the other. Conversation had in any case been easy with one who feigned enthusiastic interest in their guest's magnificent cavalry. In the President Aiku sensed the disdain of one who could never accept any superiority of forces of a still natural kind, not entirely replaced by high technology. In the eyes of this former Baltimore attorney he read ill-concealed disgust as the distant voices of the riders shouting their traditional war cries reached him. Well he knew that faint air of scorn, recalling times when he had observed the haughty Russian officers herding long lines of Mongolian shepherds towards the mines to dig for precious stones.

But when taking leave of the American leader near the steps up to his plane, Aiku had been seized by a perverse curiosity for that aircraft capable of reaching, within a few hours, a destination which he, that evening, could not possibly reach. And with a disoriented expression that only those closest to him had ever seen, he had let slip the comment that, for him, America was farther away than the moon. Even then he had not failed to observe the opposite reaction of the two American leaders: the President barely disguising his amused surprise, Halley amazed, yet moved as well. And almost as if underlining his inability to understand Aiku's disheartened realisation of being unable to dominate the course of time, the President had clapped him on the shoulder and invited him to America where, at West Point, he could see horses as magnificent as those of his famous squadron. Halley had bowed his head as if disapproving of the President's sally and had firmly shaken the Asian leader's hand before leading the American delegation into the plane.

Now, waiting there in the Belgian King's castle, Aiku was thinking of the man with whom – though they had never exchanged a word – he felt he had much in common (of that Secretary of State so disinclined to subscribe to a cynical exchange of forces, men and means) when, at last, Ethelbert and Poliakoff were announced. After hearing about the talks with the President of the United States, they told him of fresh troubles caused by atomic destruction. In the Carpathians where volcanoes, inactive for thousands of years, were again throwing up lava, rock fragments and ash, spreading them for hundreds of miles around, the vegetation had changed beyond all knowledge. They had heard of gigantic plants growing in Bucharest, plants that within a few hours had shot up to the tops of the tallest buildings, transforming the city into a strange kind of forest more resembling the Amazon jungle than the Wallachian woods. However his ministers' muttered complaints were beginning to irritate him; and feeling he could no longer bear hearing about those clearly revengeful signs of offended Nature, he dismissed the two so that at last he could be alone. Ordering a horse he set off at a gallop, jumping the low wall surrounding that coquettish, anything but military, eighteenth-century castle, and rode hard towards the plain of Waterloo, towards the farm buildings from where nearby, his magnificent squadron had rushed out in simulated attack against an imaginary enemy.

No one was about in the vicinity of Waterloo at that hour. A small granite lion, worn by time, stood on top of a slight rise in the ground, commemorating some local event, but so long ago that few of the letters remained in the inscription to tell what had happened. Oblivion shrouded the causes that had led men to remember Waterloo, nothing now remained except the name. A moment later Aiku was on the hill top where stood the lion seemingly desirous of exerting a will to maintain control beyond the calm and peaceful landscape of little Belgium. But by now it was quite dark. Far away the lights of a military base near Brussels brought the present day to mind, diminishing the time-worn figure of the lion. To Aiku those white and yellow lights shone like a challenge urging him to play his hand like all other men, ignorant of the future and indifferent to what it might bring, with no written script to guide him, trusting in the horizon bounded by the brief space of time and place which eye and hand could compass. But such was not for him; he had not left the desert to live in the world as had the American President, as blessedly ignorant as he as to the workings of his plane, abandoned to forms and complicities of present appearances, trustful and defenceless like one of the many political leaders of that world conquered by his might. Dismounting, he leant against the Waterloo lion. Who, he wondered, had really won that day at Waterloo, he or the sly and easy-going President? Supposing he himself were the winner, how long would it last? A fragment of stone fell into his hand; the lion was crumbling to bits, he could just bear being looked at but little else; even memories of the past were beyond him let alone the weight of a hand accustomed to grasping fate.

With the sensual pleasure of danger to be faced in the thick of the fight, he plunged down into the night spurring his horse, neither knowing nor caring where he went; the whole land was his now, nowhere in it would he be thought a stranger. Ethelbert, however, had already decided to sound the alarm, unleash the Urga squadron, his personal guards, to look for him when, out of the night, they heard him dash like a fury into the castle of Laeken.

Very soon, in company with the king of little Belgium, Aiku left for Vienna.

5

I N AN Austria laid low by the aftermath of a terrible
epidemic of cholera, a scourge that, after a lapse of
centuries, had reappeared following arrival of the Tartars,
the Congress of Vienna was opened.

Suddenly restored to the level of a Central European
capital, the city assumed a kind of tragicomic splendour
expressed in the half-deserted Ring resounding with the
hooves of cavalry squadrons, in the balconies of buildings
festively decorated with the flags of many nations, and in
the red velvet carpets laid down in front of the Hofburg to
welcome the foreign delegation. The Vindobona of Marcus
Aurelius, which had driven back the threatening barbarians,
the Vienna of John Sobieski, once the ultimate bastion
against the Turks, now offered hospitality to the leader of
the Tartars and the congress of his vassals. Sessions were held
at the Royal Palace of Schönbrunn where the Emperor of
Austria, firstborn of Archduke Otto, son of the last Emperor,
officially acted as host. Although Aiku, High Protector of
Europe and of the Old Continent (such was the title he
had decided to assume on opening the Congress) retained
overall control, for reasons of administrative convenience

and connections with mitteleuropa as well, he had thought it best to restore the monarchy, giving the Hapsburgs back their earlier possessions, and adding Germany now too crushed by the atom bomb to form her own government. Entering the Hofburg a few days before, everything had seemed to him ready for the resurrection he had planned.

In the vast dining hall, with all the places laid just as when the Emperor of Austria had dined there for the last time in November 1918, all was still, as if a signal were awaited from he who could order the reversal of time. In the room where audiences were held the great register still lay open at the name of Princess Melanie of Metternich, the Chancellor's elderly daughter, who had hurried to the Palace on 12 November 1918 a few hours before her sovereign renounced power, to urge Karl I "not to worry overmuch since revolutions are like floods: they sweep across the land submerging it but they do not last forever and when the water subsides the land emerges once more."

So up the wide stairway of Schönbrunn filed the shadows of those who had been the great ones of the earth, resuscitated at the whim of one who had proved stronger, thus appearing to legitimise his right. Inside and outside the Palace, units of Zungarian troops stood on guard in the blue silk uniforms they wore in summer in the Tarbagatai valleys. First there passed the Emperor of Austria and King of Hungary – his apostolic majesty – followed by the Tsar of Bulgaria, the Kings of Greece, Romania, Yugoslavia, Spain, England, Italy and, one after another, those of all the other European countries.

Then came the Shah of Persia, the Kings of Jordan, Saudi Arabia, Afghanistan, Nepal, Bhutan, the Sultans of Turkey, Oman, Kuwait and thirty maharajahs of India, the King of Morocco, the Bey of Tunisia, the Khedive of Egypt, the Negus of Ethiopia, the Senussi of Libya, the Sultan of Zanzibar and many more. Except for the few actually reigning at the time of the Tartar conquest, they had mostly been unearthed after careful search in all the countries of Europe, Asia and Africa where many were busying themselves with occupations far removed from the regal style. Last of all, just before the High Protector himself arrived, came the Tsar of All the Russias, awkward in his ceremonial dress, who had been only just discovered in Italy where he had been managing his wife's estates.

Also present were the Vice President of the United States of America and the heir to the Emperor of Japan, both invited as observers and as personal guests of the High Protector – not permitted however to attend all sessions but only those dealing with matters concerning the East, and the 'West Indies' as official language expressed it. Increasingly curious about the Empire, still warm under the ashes of Republican Austria, Aiku in a matter of days had unleashed his ministers in search of all the most erudite people available, heraldry enthusiasts, private collectors, archivists, retired professors of history in the universities with whose aid he had created the scenario against which he would act out his Congress.

With great sense of realism the first question discussed was the limits to be placed on sovereignty in the various provinces of the Empire. Pleased at finding he need not face any German compatriot in that assembly, Ethelbert had been chosen to read out the High Protector's official proposals. The states represented at the meeting would be granted a degree of sovereignty that left foreign policy, defence and economic planning in the High Protector's hands, as well as some decisions on internal policy to be made, state by state, at the meetings of the national subcommittees. Each country could mint its own coinage, print postage stamps, collect taxes half to be paid into its national exchequer, the other half into that of the High Protector. The ministers of each national government would attend to their tasks as mere administrators of their peoples, abstaining from ideological questions and political decisions on pain of overthrow of the government and of the reigning dynasty. A common army would have to be maintained by all parts of the Empire, each country providing a contingent in proportion to its population. Citizens were free to worship as they chose: those different religions, Aiku claimed, are like the five fingers of a single hand. Previous legislation and codes would remain in force unless in conflict with the decisions of the Congress. All parties, parliaments and trade unions were abolished. Ministers were to be appointed by the sovereigns, the High Protector's assent to be considered as binding; the supreme government of the Empire, aided by the Grand Council of Tartars, was to be instituted at the High Protector's headquarters from where it would control the work of the national governments. The High Protector was responsible to himself alone, and claimed the right to decide on questions of succession to the throne should the ruling dynasty come to an end. Each state should receive an annual visit from the High Protector and his train. National sovereigns were to pay a visit to the High Protector at least once a year. Three fleets were to be built: in the Baltic Sea, in the Indian Ocean and in the Atlantic. Each country must find room for a number of military bases according to its size and strategic position. Neutrality was temporarily recognised for Portugal, however, where the Congress hoped that the Braganzas would shortly be restored to the throne in the person of Don Duarte, Duke of Braganza. Concluding his exposition of fundamental principles, after a pause during which the sovereigns were careful not to comment on what they had heard, Ethelbert reconvened them all in the Hall of Mirrors.

There were more important proposals the High Protector wanted them to hear; and to prove that the same if not greater importance was attached to those now forthcoming, Aiku himself unexpectedly appeared at the head of a long table. During the last few days in Vienna he had altered his style of dress. The loose wide trousers, the short dark cloak, the turban bejewelled with a star of rubies had little by little, during the days of that lenient review of the past, given place to less oriental clothes, and he was now wearing a grey flannel jacket with gilded buttons over dark narrow trousers. But it was his head, free of its turban and showing his thick black curls, which seemed to express dignity and strength as if, devoid of exotic ornament and symbol, he exhaled an inner superiority, counting more on the consensus of those around him than on hierarchical subordination based on glitter and uniforms. The personages crowding the hall were all impressed by the change and settled down to listen to Ethelbert without taking their eyes off Aiku who now and then fixed his gaze on one or other of them, moving it from some point above their heads where he seemed desirous of giving his black eyes a rest.

Europe, said Ethelbert, had collapsed not only because of Tartar military superiority but because of the many diseases that had weakened her spirit. Born in faraway Mongolia, the High Protector could and would contribute to a moral healing of the old continent in showing obeisance to the greatness of her past. Pursuing this end, perhaps of greater importance than political unity, he asked for special help and understanding. He well knew that facing him were seated the descendants of those who had once made Europe great and strong; never should they think he meant to humiliate them by a display of power in that ancient Palace from where the ancestors of their host had issued orders to millions of men.

He prayed them to show humility in listening to the counsel and proposals offered them by the son of a shepherd from the Gobi desert, proposals no longer backed by the power of his sword but by the heart of a man concerned about his fellow men. The word barbarous should not be used in relation to his humble origins: had not the religion most widespread among them been founded by the son of an unknown carpenter of Judea, born in a cave and venerated by shepherds?

These words were rendered by Ethelbert in rather uncertain English, not because he had insufficient mastery of the language but because he was little accustomed to such heartfelt and openly conciliatory tones from his leader. While pausing to take a drink of water, Aiku could not fail to realise the embarrassment of his minister and, using his own language, he turned to the assembly addressing them with great simplicity of manner while the interpreter translated when some interruption gave him an opportunity.

"Lords of Europe, Asia and Africa", and pushing aside the pages of notes, gazing at each of his interlocutors one by one, Aiku began to improvise, "there is a great evil abroad in our world, an evil which has been the means of my victory: the atom bomb. Our mistake was to believe that happiness could be gained by imprisoning the forces of nature, a mistake that has always been the same, one that has made my people too the losers, compelled to wrest precious stones from the heart of the mountains and transform them into jewels and riches. I intend to right this wrong, to restore the world to its natural order. And together with the bomb we must prevent yet another pest from spreading: the computer. In our states we shall prohibit the use of these malignant machines that destroy all chance of error, that steal plausibility from every statement, from every bold stroke of imagination. From now on men shall not resort to machines for anything they themselves are capable of inventing alone. No school in our states shall have a single one. For similar reasons I believe you will agree with me on the advisability of limiting television to avoid men having to forgo the use of speech and bow to the tyranny of images. To the children we shall give books, drawing paper and animals. In our schools we shall try not only to instil knowledge but also to teach the cult and veneration of Nature; every child shall have a cat, dog or bird to tend, starting from the first year of school. I have learned more from the animals my people grazed in the upper Tula, than from the books I have since read. Anyone who illtreats or exploits an animal will be dealt with as if he had done it to a man!

"That is all gentlemen. But allow me to make one last recommendation. I well know that what I have said leads to one conclusion only, to freedom from my iron hand, to achievement of a conscience liberated from the servitude that in the bottom of your hearts you cannot but hate. The never-ending destruction of these recent months proclaims the detestable nature of my victories. And if in what I have said, in the requests I have made, there is something of importance for you, in the end I must surely be eliminated by a Europe arising from the ashes I myself have spread. There is no greater service I could render to the world than that of bringing hate upon myself for having imposed with violence that love of good which your people, in the full moral and political freedom they enjoyed, had forgotten how to love by inventing the atrocious invincibility of the atom bomb and the artificial brain. There is a mysterious contradiction in things which neither you nor I can solve; how it is that, while enjoying freedom, we not only find it impossible to love that condition, but seem impelled to do all we can to return to a state of affairs where no freedom exists.

"I am no admirer of your institutions, mark that well; I abhor the weakness of democracy, the limited utility of assemblies, their slowness, the solemn lie of equality. Yet I feel with all my strength that, in some place on a higher level than is possible for a man born where reigns the beauty of mountains and deserts, the value of such institutions can be understood and appreciated; they shall be sacred as the flowers, as children, as the birds in the sky. You are monarchs, part of an order, as am I, belonging more to nature than to history, of origins more distant than are those of democratic institutions, sons of a principle of superiority in battle that, centuries ago, made you kings. Do not be hostile to me; help me."

Concluding his speech Aiku wondered how many of those sovereigns, restored to their positions by the Congress, were not – already and irremediably – sons of their times, tainted by the mentality he had stigmatised to their faces. He well knew that, as private citizens, many of them had earned their living producing just those machines whose use he wanted to suppress.

Complete silence had fallen on the great Hall of Mirrors of Schönbrunn. The High Protector had been speaking while daylight started to wane. A prompt hand somewhere in the Palace pressed a switch and the light of the Bohemian lamps, a present to Marie Thérèse from the Prague municipality, was reflected a thousand times in the mirrors, instantly dispelling the tense and unreal atmosphere that Aiku's words had evoked. Ethelbert's surprise was evident and, while polishing his glasses with a tired expression, his anxious glance moved here and there among the crowd of kings.

None of them, it seemed, intended to be the first to speak. Furtively they looked around each trying to guess from others' faces who would dare do so, each hoping he could later suit

51

his attitude to Aiku's humour. They had all understood his
words, having listened to the interpreter's English translation,
but very few had understood the man himself. The uneasiest
among them seemed the Emperor of Austria whose chivalrous
sense of hospitality imposed upon him the duty of speaking
first, but so confused were his ideas that he could think of
nothing particular to say. What designs did that man have?
Was he pretending, dissimulating? How could anyone believe
such words, even though not without some nobility here and
there, and revealing a strange love for the earth he had
trampled on and devastated? At that very moment, bringing
to mind the terrible epidemic of cholera, a wail of ambulances
could be heard through the open windows; another wound
inflicted on the nation by those cursed orientals. How could
one believe him? Who did that mysterious man want people
to think he was?

The first to speak was the new Tsar of All the Russias,
who, born in France, had never seen the country over
which he had been placed to reign. (He knew Russian
and maintained he had always been able to talk with his
people when Russian emigrants gathered round him once
a year at Easter.) He thanked the High Protector for his
noble words and then started such a long series of objections
that the Congress stenographers could barely keep pace
with him. They were rather futile points, quibbles about
national sovereignty, requests for greater autonomy, proposals
for territorial adjustments, movement of border lines. All
matters, thought Aiku, that could have been raised in a
congress held a century earlier. Like a spectre, the Balkan
question once again appeared, then the problem of the
Baltic Republics, protection of orthodox Slavs, the need
to keep watch at the Straits of Bosphorus over Turkey
who had raised her head when the Russian catastrophe

had occurred. When the Tsar spoke of the need for certain territorial compensation to the West, where Poland did not seem sufficiently strong, the King of Poland rose in protest at this yet further threat to his country; and insults were exchanged between the two new sovereigns who had not even met each other. The Tsar of Bulgaria, faced with reductions to his territory in favour of Greece, protested that under such conditions his sovereignty could not be guaranteed and, approaching the Sultan of Turkey, began talking to him with all too eloquent cordiality. The Emperor of Austria, until a week earlier earning his living with his brother-in-law Michael of Romania selling aeroplanes to Arabia and Persia, sought to prove to the High Protector that it was not so certain that all machines prevented people from thinking, that aeroplanes were not as harmful to humanity as were computers. He was supported by the Sultan of Zanzibar who held half the shares in an English helicopter factory and suggested destroying trains instead, since they had now become too slow.

But the noisiest were the Arabian rulers; Ethelbert was therefore obliged to call them to order, and ask them to speak one at a time. None of them could forgo their riches from oil; dollar payments from many developed countries were still outstanding. The peaceful African leaders, offended because Aiku had not mentioned them in his speech, on hearing from the Governor of Aden and the Bey of Tunis about the Waterloo meeting, woke up and began shouting. Who, demanded the Bey impudently, had won at Waterloo? Was it true that nothing more could be exported to America and that the old continent would be unable to obtain anything more from the United States? The servants outside the forty doors – the number opening into that hall chosen to allow nearly all the sovereigns to enter simultaneously so as to solve the problem of precedence – feared they would have to intervene and separate some of the most angry.

When the Maharaja of Nagpur caused an affront to the Maharaja of Indore by posing the still unsettled question of the Sikh religion, the clamour raised by the other twenty-eight maharajas was so violent that the High Protector was compelled to speak.

Not one of them, he said, had shown any real concern for the future, for the ills even then disturbing the climate, polluting the waters, causing such monstrous deterioration. No-one had considered his proposals for a reborn world. They had merely resorted to unworthy shouting as if nothing had happened, as if their new evils added to the former ones made up a single whole, in the face of which they would carry on as before. Perhaps deep down they wanted him to remedy matters after causing so much destruction, perhaps none of them really wanted to help; perhaps they had actually taken him seriously and hated him as he had expected they would.

To him, however, it seemed a selfish hate, lacking in foresight – a hate without generosity, without love for their peoples, aimed merely at ensuring they would more or less regain their old privileges. A few of the most impudent were acting as if he had appeared in the firmament of history solely to restore to them their former rights. Perhaps he had wronged Africa and Asia in showing so much concern for Europe, as if those ancient lands deserved more consideration than others. Clearly he could expect little help from them for his plan for that back-to-nature world he dreamed of and had revealed in his speech, in which evil – his own domination – would be at the service of good. That meant they had taken his words as those of the barbarous warrior they wanted him to be. But now, no proposal other than those he had put forward was to be placed on the agenda. They were asked to take note of his decision concerning world government already explained by Ethelbert, sign the agreement and return to their capitals to execute, and have executed, the orders he had given.

Anyone daring to betray him would lose not only his crown but his life. Those in disagreement could forgo their titles and leave as soon as possible for the land where, by long tradition, dissidents received political asylum: the United States of America.

6

THE CARS shot to and fro around the great black limousine just as on any working day in June. Traffic was heavy as usual, flowing smoothly in the familiar Washington. James, the chauffeur, invariably appeared reserved and discreet, with his shiny bald head and crown of black hair. That morning too he had handed his master the financial and other newspapers with his habitual smile before opening the door of the official car for him. The car telephone had rung three times to remind him of morning engagements, beginning with the ten o'clock meeting at the White House. The neat houses of the capital, the straight and tidy roads he had so often seen as he rapidly passed along, the on-off lighted signs in the square – everything seemed to reflect the same tranquil order of things. For the first time Halley remarked to himself that in all those years he had never walked along those roads, seen them only as he hurried by, more distant than the stars, farther from reach, more forbidden than any Garden of Eden. Barely time enough to pass through them in the car – and fast too, not to miss an important government appointment, a fleeting vision of branches and leaves, sometimes fallen on the ground,

56

sometimes of a fresh green: the seasons had become a matter of stolen glances, just perceptible while the eye sought the news on the printed pages and the ear listened to the telephone. So too would pass what remained of his life, closed in his man-of-the-government box, every movement and gesture counted out as if by clockwork; already fifty years of those gestures had gone by, and there was nothing to promise anything different. He ordered James to stop. Amazed, his chauffeur looked back at the Secretary of State, fearing he had misunderstood.

"Here James, I said. Stop here and wait for me." A few yards more and James brought the limousine to a halt. Looking in the mirror to let a few cars go by, he waited for the right moment to get out and open the door for Halley. But Halley was before him, getting out by himself alongside the trees, leaving the car door open. That was strange. Here was his elegant master walking among the trees, peering among their lower branches, touching them even; now he had stopped and was staring up as if there was something at the top . . . Why had he stopped? Although James had been with his master for seven years, there had always been surprises; he was hard to understand, always alone whenever he could get away from government business; no vices, no friends, so different from the others he had driven all over America . . . Always so kind but reserved, those eyes seemingly constrained by some outside force, like horses being trained to keep a foot pace, held back on a short rein. Especially when he was looking at a woman . . .

But what had made him want to stop? It was risky just there, not allowed; the police would be along at any moment. And now he was touching the trunks, turning and looking back . . . James began to feel rather nervous. It was not the first time his master had had these sudden changes of humour, rather bewildering as if there were another Halley inside him, the one as impatient as the other was disciplined, the one eccentric and the other so impassive . . .

Halley's wish was to break down that invisible wall raised up between his mornings on government business and Nature so enclosed within the city's geometrical layout. At that moment he was contemplating his life from a standpoint contradictory to the one he had maintained for years. Above the roar of the traffic he could, for the first time, faintly but clearly, distinguish the rushing sound of the Potomac river passing under the bridge only a short distance away, it too a prisoner of bridges and roads, it too sucked up into a synthesis of streets and buildings, expressways and underpassess; but still alive, perhaps ready to rebel and one day overflow its banks, unleashing all its force like a vendetta for its long imprisonment. His thoughts returned to the man from Mongolia, to the force of *his* vendetta – that of Nature outraged in its most intimate and sacred laws. Thus had Halley perceived him, had done so ever since their meeting at Waterloo with the President. The events of that occasion had destroyed in him what remaining confidence he had felt in the President's policy, a light had been lit that had altered the course of his whole life and could not be extinguished. And now that he himself was on his way to sanction a monstrous condominium of the earth, more than ever he felt how hard it would be to keep silent, to pretend he still subscribed to the spirit and the letter of that accord. He often saw through the windows of the car the statue of Lincoln seated before the white mass of the Capitol; had he died that his country might reach such cynicism, when he had led it through weary civil war to build a less racist society?

The only thing worse than the pact itself was the in-difference with which public opinion in the United States appeared to have accepted it. Apart from a few small groups of intellectuals, opponents for ever relegated by common consent to a ghetto of those considered 'different', not a single voice had spoken up, in Congress and in the two main parties, to reject it and suggest defending Europe. In a television message the American President had quite easily persuaded a people too wishful of carrying on its untroubled existence to protest. And the matter ended there, with the sight of the President's pale smiling face resting on his usual white collar and grey tie, saying good evening to his people, collecting up with studied slowness the pages of his speech from the reading desk, decorated with the presidential coat of arms, while the notes of the national anthem proffered reassuring words of peace accompanied by the usual roll of drums. But could the contemptible evasion of responsibility announced by that message really be peace?

Just then Halley pricked his finger on the bark of a tree. A red drop oozed from under the nail of his forefinger. Once again he gazed at the river harnessed within its banks like the blood under his skin. Once again he was aware of some presentiment, as if the equilibrium of his body and that of nature were so fragile and temporary as to be upset even by a slight scratch. But hark, there were the police sirens; as he had expected they were coming to protest and ask him to proceed on his way. The car should not have stopped along that road. He glanced at his watch: seven minutes' disobedience, that was all they had allowed him. The way they kept order in that prison was certainly most efficient. People really had learned they must never stop. By some instinctive association of ideas he wondered why Aiku had stopped his forward march; what fear had he felt in Italy? But the two policemen were now beside him and, on recognising the President's Secretary of State, withdrew a few yards waiting in respectful silence for the car to restart. Halley got in, under the alarmed eyes of James, sucking his finger that still bled a little. The long black car gathered speed preceded by the police, the wailing siren leading the way so that he could make up for lost time. Halley's attention, however, was taken up by his finger although it had stopped bleeding, as if that moment of freedom and irregular behaviour had never been.

The White House appeared; there was the usual ceremony of recognition and checking, then the car rolled slowly along the main drive watched by plain clothes men. There were the last of the cabinet members hurrying in. Again he was struck by the mechanical nature of their gestures, by those bodies always clothed in the same style, walled within their own forms, like everything he had seen when, just earlier, he had left his car, moving yet imprisoned. For no reason once again he wondered why Aiku had stopped; he personified freedom from form; it was not in him to stop and because of that he had won. So what on earth could have happened? In Aiku's place he himself would not have stopped . . . It amazed him that for an instant he had thought of himself as Aiku. But here were his colleagues to bring him back to reality. Climbing the stairs to the Oval Office he realised that those seven minutes' delay did not even exist. He entered, made his greetings and received them, taking his seat besides the President who shortly after began to speak.

"Well my friends, at Waterloo we won. I really can say I have ensured a long period of peace for my country and America." And the rest of the world? wondered Halley. After a brief pause the President continued, "Just as I thought, that savage is not trying to pick a quarrel, he wants to live in peace, leaving America and business with Japan to us." The President went on to explain details of the agreement: Portuguese neutrality, cession of England and Spain, the promise America had made not to interfere in revolutionary movements in Africa, the expansion of Japan at the expense of Indonesia, the Philippines and Australia.

"Taking it all in all we should be grateful to the Tartars! In less than two years of war they have freed us from the threat of Russia – no small matter you will admit . . . And then there's no knowing how long he will be able to keep his position. Europe is facing disaster. On the way from Brussels airport to Waterloo they did all they could to use roads away from the towns and villages, keeping the blinds down so that I shouldn't see anyone, but I saw those poor creatures . . . Spectres they were, not people, frightfully thin. The effects of the bomb are spreading all over, read this . . ." and one of the secretaries handed round copies of a report that had just arrived with a map of the countries where atomic radiation had begun to spread.

"But they are getting organised at Vienna; he has called a meeting of all those phoney kings to tell them what to do. If he manages to handle such a vast empire it's hard to say whether the Russians as they used to be were more to be feared than are Aiku's Tartars now," commented the Secretary for Defence, who liked to be the first to speak at Cabinet meetings.

"That's something else I wanted to talk to you about after the Waterloo agreement", said the President lowering his tone and assuming a mysterious expression as if alluding to some hidden truth, before he went on to explain other less important questions discussed with Aiku as a kind of preamble to what he had to say. Then at last, raising his voice, he continued, "As far as the Vienna Congress is concerned, it seems he made some unacceptable proposals to start and then advanced such absurd arguments that not even those kings could take him seriously."

There had been silence in the room, but at the President's words a murmur of surprise arose. As if anticipating their questions and smiling in his swivel chair, he resumed, "Yes, only the son of a Mongolian shepherd who grew up in the mountains and deserts could suggest to a Europe on her knees and to an enslaved Asia and Africa that machinery, computers, atomic weapons, technology should all be destroyed, that television should be done away with, that a kitten should be given to each child at school instead of a calculator."

At this a few cabinet members laughed, others put questions, some wanted to know if they had got it quite straight. Only Halley appeared impassive, his head bent over his papers.

"Gentlemen, I can assure you, he actually did say that. But there's more to come, as I said, even more incredible . . ." The President smiled again, pausing to enjoy the sight of an audience begging him to continue.

"He asked his vassals to hate him, to help him in his task of freeing the world from the atom bomb and machines, by their renewed regard for nature, forgotten because of . . . us. Yes, because it was we who tainted the world with scientific progress!"

At this the members' comments became even more hilarious. A few guffawed, omitting to take note of points of more importance for their work and their departments. Only Halley, the white-haired Secretary of State seated on the President's right, looked more and more solemn taking no part in the general good humour, but fixing his gaze at some point above the heads of his colleagues. Could it be that the scene before him brought to mind a picture of the

Pharoah of Egypt's court when, together with their lord, the courtiers burst into lewd and rowdy laughter – of which they were one day to repent – before Moses who had come with the Jewish leaders to request freedom for his people? He had accompanied the President to Waterloo, had met the man who now, in Europe, had taken for himself the name of High Protector, a title stimulating yet kindly – with something vaguely Cromwellian about it. The man was by no means stupid, he thought, quite the contrary; neither did he share his chief's presumptuous optimism and superficial opinions. Just at that moment the politician of distant British origin – descendant of Edmund Halley, the astronomer, whose name was linked to the comet discovered in 1682 during a voyage to the island of St. Helena – remembered his father.

Many times during his brilliant career had his father, a Calvinist clergyman, warned him against the pragmatism of the Republican party and the easy-going attitude of the Democrats, in long arguments when the old man would chide his son, especially about the policy of denying protection to Europe.

"Believe me, if that madman were to give us back a Europe defenceless and without technology a few years hence, we would not have to spend one dollar to regain power over her and chase that shepherd back to his flocks in the Gobi desert."

"But that's what he wants, Mr. President. That's just what he wants!" Halley exclaimed, unable any longer to hide the embarrassment he felt for his chief, and rose so suddenly from the chair that pages of notes slid onto the table. He seemed almost a different man; and his snowy hair, always so carefully combed, had become ruffled by his unusual state of agitation, and framed a face of austere severity, which bore the expression more of an ancient patriarch than a thoughtful and serious Secretary of State.

"If, after Aiku, Europe returns to her past, she will reject us too! Fighting against his tyranny she will learn to hate all tyrannies, even that of her past allies and masters. They won't want us any more. Our arms are like those Aiku possesses, exactly the same as his!"

No longer amused, the members were now animatedly exchanging opinions, commenting on the Secretary of State's words, raising objections. Few appeared to accept the views expressed by that disturbing presence; most showed opposition and bewildered surprise as if the ghost of a guilty past, unpleasant to admit but hard to deny, stood among them. For his part, the President used his impassive expression to ally himself with the intangible hostility of his cabinet, stopped rocking his chair and waited for silence to return to the Oval Office. He had no intention of commenting in front of them on what Halley had said; he preferred to avoid extending the discussion which might stray onto uncontrollable ground. Halley, his Secretary of State, should have been more careful, have kept quiet and not have so openly contradicted his chief just then; he could have done it in private if he really had to. All the same the President thought it best not to show annoyance; it might be counter-productive and consolidate some uncertain opinions.

"Gentlemen, I think that is all I have to tell you today about Waterloo and the Vienna Congress. Our next appointment will be tomorrow at five p.m. for the usual Wednesday meeting."

Left alone with Halley, however, the President returned to the question of Europe, protesting at the strange attitude his Secretary of State had assumed. What had he meant to say? Perhaps to declare America's guilt before the whole world?

Did he think it was the right time to indulge in sophisticated and philosophical soul-searching? And just after the kind of disaster they had contemplated together in Europe? What was to be done if not come to terms with that ruffian and hope for his rapid downfall to restore the previous state of balance? He did not believe his Secretary of State could really think that they, the Americans, had called forth that scourge, conjured up that spectre . . . The discussion went on and on, becoming more and more inflamed. Though of the same party, there was profound disagreement between the two over a problem that, for the one, was not strictly political while, for the other, it was and would have to remain a question exclusively pertaining to foreign policy. At one moment when the atmosphere had become really tense, Halley, who was shortsighted, took out his pocket handkerchief to wipe his glasses. While doing so, he glanced up at the wall behind the President where hung the great oil portraits of George and Martha Washington: in their plump rosy faces – he under a cascade of fluffy white curls, she wearing the white cap of the fertile spouse – he thought for an instant that he saw the kindly and simple parents of that simple son. But it lasted only a moment until, putting on his spectacles again, vision and verity were restored to him. The man sitting before Halley's pitiless glasses once more became the President while the two portraits resumed their dignity as progenitors of the fatherland, as legends of the glorious thirteen colonies once strong enough to weaken the tyranny of George III, mad King of England.

They parted about ten o'clock at night, neither having felt he could attempt to approach the other's point of view. Aiku is already here, thought Halley, he has crossed the ocean, his comic Congress is becoming a serious matter for us too, I'm sure of it. His thoughts reverted to that moment just before he and the President left when the Tartar leader had revealed the insane yet extraordinary spirit of the insatiable conqueror, that moment when he wondered what the air would be like in New York that evening, air that he himself would not be able to breathe. Halley reflected on the significance which the appearance of so simple yet mysterious a man might have at that precise moment in history. Why not before? What strategy lay behind his move to share world power with the head of the United States? The world was too small to contain a lust for power like that, there was no room for two masters in his plans for domination. Clearly his move was part of a much more complex and far-reaching scheme.

Two powers will always clash. Aiku had not set out with the intention of stopping and then of sharing the world with another. He most surely had chosen to defeat America in some battle now deferred, a battle different from anything the American President had thought he would have to face. Not by the use of arms, no, but by going back into history to an order of things which restored human consciences to a better, less diabolical world. Lately scenes from the Bible had come back to mind, taught him when a child by his father: the descendants of Cain – Jabal, Silla and Tubal-Cain – "they who work iron and bronze, who beat copper and iron". "The Cainites, men who brought about material progress," his father used to say in his teachings from the Book of Genesis, "remember, they are still among us. They are the sons of evil, the men of progress, the sons of Cain, never forget . . ."

Growing up he had often felt ashamed of the cultural conservatism of the Presbyterian pastor who had never abandoned his study of the scriptures, even in conflict with the Synod who would have preferred him to show greater willingness to comprehend the needs of the souls entrusted to his care in the small town near Washington where he lived.

The years Halley had spent studying economy at Palo Alto, then further years of activity in the Democratic party until he was elected Senator and occupied the prestigious position of Secretary of State, had merely widened the gap between father and son. But for some time now, in fact since Aiku had appeared on the horizon and events had taken such a dramatic turn, Halley once again had felt the fascination of those words of ancient times that his father never tired in all his life of believing as the only true ones. After experiencing for so many years a thirst for knowledge and scientific progress as in the myth of Prometheus, he now felt strangely attracted by the negative legend of Cain – the other perspective of the same historical situation of his country. But never before had he seen the problem so clearly as on that evening after the cabinet meeting in the White House, after his argument with the President seated in front of the portraits of George and Martha Washington; the stupid fellow had not understood what was happening on the other side of the ocean, in the lands lying between America and Japan.

7

I N HIS study the old Emperor of Japan peered through
the microscope at a new vegetable species which a famous
botanist, Baron Höbner, Austrian Ambassador to Japan, had
brought him from Europe a few days before. In the studies
he made of vegetable life, the refuge from world politics
he had always sought, there now appeared before the old
man's eyes a historical truth which a scientist such as he
could not avoid. Those terrible plants from the area around
Bucharest in Romania were not typical of any climate on
earth; as far as he knew there was no place where temperature
and atmospheric pressure could permit such dizzy growth of
vegetable fibres, such prodigious and violent strength, fleshy
colour and consistency.

In recent days the Prime Minister had been telling him how
things were going in Europe, of the turn of events so strangely
favourable for Japan. He had listened, as for seventy-two
years the Emperor of Japan had impassively listened to his
government's political announcements, in his black tunic,
upright at his desk, below the portrait of his father, the
insane Emperor whose functions, when not even twenty
years old, he had assumed as regent, oppressed ever since

68

by a feeling of guilt. In that same room seventy years ago they had come to make him sign the treaty with Hitler and with Mussolini, later the declaration of war against France, Britain and, finally, against the United States. In that same room the Commander-in-Chief of the Imperial troops had thrown himself in tears at his feet, imploring pardon for his soldiers who had lost the war. And while the Emperor had turned his back and looked through the window at his garden, the Commander had committed hara-kiri – imitated shortly after by all his superior officers. During the subsequent tranquil years of his symbolic power, heads of state had come on official visits, their prime ministers opening entire world markets to Japanese economic penetration. But no force in that convulsive world where so many, gesticulating wildly, proclaimed their invincibility before shuddering in the final spasm of death, no such force had ever reached the depths of his private world of study. His father had astutely used a mask of insanity as a shield against the impossible burden of power. He himself had used science to mark the confines of his freedom. However now some phenomenon had appeared to override all limits. And he, over ninety, could still see . . .

If those eyes, which remembered the many dead in this century, could only have closed before perceiving what was now beneath their gaze, his long reign would have been lived through to perfection. As a boy, heir to the throne, he had played billiards with the last Tsar, had gone riding with the Kaiser, had corresponded with Edward VII, the son of Queen Victoria. His life had indeed been a long one . . . almost as if plants had endowed him with their longevity. Perhaps his son, whose constitution was not so good and who had now reached seventy, would not even manage to succeed him, heir for life to a father so beloved by his people as to be irreplaceable. And then, his grandchildren gave promise of rapidly adapting to the roles of all modern heads of state, American and European. Thus would his legend finally disappear, absorbed within the demoniacal aptitude of Japan to imitate those in dominating position, adapting to models far removed from those of their own country. The Prime Minister had pointed out that once again the nation could benefit from misfortune, transform evil into good. The atomic explosion that had struck Russia, eliminating her from the group of powers dangerous to Japan and causing millions of Chinese to move westwards, would allow Japan to expand towards the Philippines and Indonesia, perhaps one day even towards India, certainly towards Australia. As on previous occasions he had had to sign a declaration of war and, a week later, receive the representatives of the defeated who had offered him a new crown. The United States Ambassador had then come for an audience bringing a letter of congratulations from his President. So now, after nearly fifty years, accounts were equal: the American who, following defeat was to have deposed him, now sought closer friendship, pressed for secret understandings, for more promising connections. Everything always in the name of money, that money which his secretaries said was so plentiful, they hardly knew how to calculate the interest that flowed in daily on sums deposited in various parts of the world. In recent months events had proceeded so fast that he could not devote more than an hour or two a day to his botanical research. The world was shaken, its joints creaked like a building during an earthquake.

Incredible news had arrived from Europe. The Mongol warrior Aiku had occupied it and, in Vienna, had arranged a Congress of his vassals on whom he intended to impose his will. Now, in his Imperial government's protocols, in diplomatic relations and in the credentials he had to receive from each new ambassador, it seemed that the clock of history had been turned back, resuscitating corpses of ancient sovereignty, of royalty attacked and killed in cold blood, like the Russian Imperial family. Strange indeed was it for the Emperor of Japan, the only one still reigning to hold that title, to find among the ambassadors' papers names such as the Emperor of Austria, the Tsar of Russia, the Kings of Italy and of Romania . . . Had he been able to close his eyes during certain audiences, it might have seemed as if he were living in the hot summer of 1914 . . . But the world was not made up of names alone, just as it was not only made of money. Behind those names lay the rigid control of a single master, Aiku. And, hidden behind that attention to money, explaining every political move made by his government, lay the spirit of his own people – active, hard-working, never still, renouncing the opposing tendency, that capacity for contemplation, which, almost as a counterweight to pragmatism, had so often appeared in the history of his country. A capacity which he himself had been obliged to cultivate since he could never permit himself any other behind his mask of semi-divinity.

The advantage of his age lay in the little concern he need feel for the future; what future could a patriarch of nearly a hundred possibly discern? For this very reason, however, he had been more than usually alarmed when, that morning, he had made a discovery that obliged him to pay attention to a future which, though no longer for him, had even so begun to open under his own eyes. That day, two years ago, when they had come to tell him that another atom bomb had been dropped on the world, after the one that had destroyed his own country in August 1945, he had been less alarmed than now, this morning at the microscope with the tangible signs of catastrophe under his eyes, and held in his old hands. For in his way he had loved plants better than people, with the love bestowed on forms of life that know no betrayal, that keep their place, that do not alter their opinion, humour, faith, that stay silent and watch, neglecting no detail. He knew that sensibility and 'feeling' were higher, nobler, and more absolute than 'action'. Feeling had been the scheme of things for him, his mode of living, with an avoidance of the trap of passion or the deception of ideologies.

Upon himself he had imposed a sort of primary function, never compromised therefore never degraded. Men thought they could define that condition as brutish, primitive; but he knew that plants possessed within them an ancient dignity, a phase of pristine life as fascinating as a buried Egyptian or Babylonian city could be for an archeologist. The Emperor of Japan had sought in plants that part of man which did not yield to the pernicious will to live, to be mortally present in history: had he been able to teach that impassive yet most tender love for the cosmos, he would have believed himself the greatest ruler of his dynasty, even though no member of his dynasty was more repelled than he by ambitions of glory. Only compassion for living forms had carried him through life. Now the grass-filled pillow he had always used, instead of one filled with wool, could no longer send him to sleep like a child, freeing his each night from the weight of some of his days, as one is freed from cares and remorse, each night learning something of oblivion until reaching the great darkness of the final one. Now the grass was contaminated; the bomb had conquered even that most ancient kingdom of Nature.

The day after, early in that hottest of summers, great was the emotion in Japan at the news of his death.

8

YES, DIVINE Providence had come to his aid. God had not willed that His vicar face martyrdom to halt the scourge He had sent down to punish the arrogance of men. So reasoned Leo XIV in his private study in Rome on reading a long letter from Cardinal Montenuovo, Papal Nuncio in Vienna, where Aiku the High Protector was busy discussing, and imposing, a new order on half the world held in his power. Leaning back in his chair and laying the letter down on his desk, the Pope allowed his gaze to wander through the windows thinking over what he had just learned.

Aiku had requested the hand of the Emperor of Austria's daughter, eighteen-year-old Archduchess Marie Christine, causing great embarrassment to her father and his entourage, and jealous gnashing of teeth among all the sovereigns gathered in Vienna. Cardinal Montenuovo became almost lyrical in describing how it had all happend one evening in July during a reception and ball held by the Emperor of Austria at Schönbrunn. It had soon been observed that Aiku could not take his eyes off the young Archduchess. Dressed in a splendid blue silk gown she had stayed close beside the Princess of Windisch-Graetz and appeared more interested in the night and the garden, seen through the windows opened wide onto the terrace, than in the crowded ballroom. It was known that sometime during the evening Aiku had left the Negus of Ethiopia, Asfa Wossen, and, approaching the Archduchess's Lady-in-waiting, had requested an introduction to her Imperial Highness. Blushing violently, the girl had followed him out onto the terrace from where many fragments of their conversation had been overheard by the Princess Windisch-Graetz, accustomed to that kind of duty. Who would have thought that the Tartar warrior could behave with such delicacy towards a young girl?

Using her own language which he had started to learn, he had talked to her of moonlit nights in the desert, of wailing dirges sung to the moon by the shepherds pleading that she should no longer show them that sad face but would appear happy; he had told her of his father who, on the island of Sakhalin, had served a rich merchant for ten years in order to win his beautiful daughter in marriage; of the desert flowers that bloomed for only one night, but were more lovely than those that opened by day; of the strange indolence of trees and plants at home where they took longer than anywhere else in the world to put on leaves, doing so only once in two years; of the leafless spring, melancholic like a child whose hair is already white and, following after each flowering spring, causing much sadness among the animals; of his mother brought there from Sakhalin by his father in defiance of the village soothsayer, who forecast her death if she came to the desert and fame for untold centuries because of her son. And again about his mother whom he had never seen, she having died in childbirth in Mongolia, so no one had ever been able to draw her portrait. And yet again about

74

his mother, finally asking her through his tears if she would agree to marriage to give him a daughter that might show him that unknown face.

The report, recognised by the Pope as the most moving document he had received for years from his legates, went on to say that the young Marie Christine had unhesitatingly accepted the offer. In Cardinal Montenuovo's view, such touching docility might be attributed to the fact that, like Aiku, Marie Christine was an orphan who had lost her mother at birth.

The embarrassment felt next day by her father, the Emperor of Austria, had been very great indeed; he had barely concealed his disgust not only at having to give in marriage to that Mongol a woman belonging to one of the most ancient families in Europe, but also at the hasty behaviour of his daughter who had not even awaited the paternal consent. It was known that father and daughter had argued the matter for a long time, actually in the presence of the Papal Nuncio who had been immediately informed on account of Aiku's readiness to solemnise the marriage should the father's answer be the same as his daughter's. Now they were only asking for the Holy Father's approval though everyone knew it would be hard to find any reason for preventing the wedding.

Leo XIV took twenty-four hours for reflection. This union would be of service to God; its sons would give rise to a race that would rule a new world, that should be welcomed at once into the bosom of the Church so that the words of this new kingdom on earth, an earth whose wounds would one day heal, might be inspired by the love of Christ. The Emperor of Austria must accept the sacrifice as he had accepted the throne from Aiku's hands. There must be some good in a man who was so moved at the thought of his country, of the mother he had never seen. And what simplicity he had shown in asking for a daughter? Not for a son, like anyone in the west, thought the Pope. Not like these Europeans who at once wanted a son to whom they could transfer their power, their strength, and their gods, in a word their evil egoism, but a daughter so that in some way his mother could live again. What refinements Europe had to learn from the East . . . From there the Pope's thoughts turned with sadness to the Emperor of Japan, just lately dead; the mild, contemplative patriarch he had met on one of his journeys, striking in his frail absent-minded dignity, in his gentle almost whispered words. The Pope wondered sometimes if Christ would not have found some place in the East better able to comprehend his love for men, instead of here, in Rome. Why had Peter turned towards Rome and not towards Mesopotamia, that earthly garden of ancient times between the two rivers? Two days later the Pope gave his beloved son, his catholic and apostolic majesty the Emperor of Austria, his fatherly consent to the marriage which he personally was prepared to bless in Vienna. The news greatly comforted the embarrassed Emperor who himself took the reply to the High Protector at Schönbrunn.

For the last two days Aiku had experienced a strange sensation of suspended feeling. He was aware that marriage could be dangerous since it placed a limit on future conquests of power, and the task of transforming millions of soldiers into a peaceful force, of a relatively inactive kind, would be extremely difficult after so many sensational military achievements; not only that – those he had defeated would be sharing power with him. He recalled the hard words spoken by Subotai at the Grand Council in Moscow warning him against coming to terms with the conquered.

But for Aiku there was no alternative. He was no longer free of his inner self. The charming figure of Marie Christine in her long blue silk gown, a diadem of brilliants in her hair, gazing out into the darkness from the windows opened wide onto the terrace, as if searching for her uncertain future among the stars in a cloudless sky, obsessed him day and night. It was his desire that this fragile creature should become the happy future of a new world, as if from the womb of this girl of ancient lineage could come forth a line of descendants as long-lasting as her own, projecting his power as warrior and conqueror beyond the sorrowful present of death and destruction into the figure of his daughter. Because for Aiku only a woman, a real mother of the earth, could save the world from the male tendency towards self-annihilation. In this he recognised the limits of his own life, as if an original sin, his virility, had besmirched his action. Perhaps the sin was not only his, perhaps many centuries earlier the balance had been overthrown when a man had usurped the earthly power of a woman. After prophesying that his march would end before an impassable river, the shaman of Urga had dismissed him in a way he had never forgotten:

"Oh thou, born of woman, cause of the death of thy mother, from thy loins shall come forth the great mother . . ."

Indeed, during a halt in the Steppes of Hunger, by Lake Baikal, a gypsy who read all their hands refused to read his, running away as if frightened out of her wits. He had made them go after her and drag her back before him only to hear her shout,

"I cannot, no, I cannot read your future!"

He had threatened her with death, pressed by growing uneasiness but, slipping from the grasp of her guards, she had whispered in his ear,

"I cannot . . . In your hand there is no future . . . you and the female within you." And as if driven beyond herself she had begun to flatter and coax him, offering unseemly caresses

77

and blandishments as if only an embrace could save both herself and him from the horrors threatening them. From that day he had felt unease at the sight of his bare body in the mirror as if that form, that undoubted virility, declared the presence of another creature that fed upon his life.

Now, when the Emperor of Austria was announced, for the first time in many years, a shiver of fear passed through him as if some event, entirely independent of his will, were coming to fulfilment, and he was faced with the risk of depending on others rather than on himself. So when the smiling fifty-year-old Emperor informed him that official consent had been given, and that the Pope in person was coming to conduct the wedding, Aiku, strangely touched, embraced his future father-in-law in silence. For an instant the image of his own father trudging his lonely way along a caravan route through the Gobi desert flashed through his mind, clouding his intense joy, but immediately Marie Christine, in all her splendid vitality, appeared to dispel the shadows.

Together Aiku and Marie Christine decided on a date for the wedding, to be attended by nearly all the sovereigns of the three continents still present for the Congress. No one seemed happier than the couple who, for the time being, proposed to live in the city, the place of their meeting. Ethelbert, Poliakoff and Zeja, however, insisted that they should leave immediately after the wedding to avoid giving any other conquered province an impression of special favours conferred upon the Emperor of Austria. Indeed, after the wedding had been announced, Aiku began to notice his father-in-law's ministers trying their best to secure changes to the clauses on limited sovereignty. Towards other ministers they were adopting an air of superiority that he could not permit without damaging his position as High Protector throughout the old continent. He gave his father-in-law to understand that those ministers would have to be removed unless he wanted to worsen his situation by losing Hungary which, at a stroke of the pen, could once more become a province of Russia.

As to his place of residence Aiku did not wish to discuss this with anyone though he listened to all the suggestions made. From faraway Mongolia his lieutenant, the faithful Jaba, sent him not only valuable furs as a wedding present but earnest prayers from all his people begging him to return home with his wife and rule the world from there. Subotai, governing for him in Russia as minister of the new Tsar, proposed that he should reside in Moscow, the central point of that Euroasiatic dominion where, eight hundred years before, another Tartar, Tamerlane, had made his home for some time after setting fire to the city. Vitim and Ude strongly insisted that he should have no fixed residence but should move about all over the lands he had conquered, thereby at least maintaining his tradition of warrior and wanderer. "The world", they said, "must everywhere continue to see you appear when least expected. That is the advice your father and grandfather would have given you . . ."

But Aiku said nothing about his plans, not even to Marie Christine who showed no curiosity as to where they would live. What gave her more concern was the shocking news received from various parts of Europe. There were those seventeen 'twins' in Bucharest, now a year old but little taller than a hand's breadth, who did not grow yet were very healthy. They were unusually precocious; two had learned to speak perfectly and all seemed able to adapt to a world of giants like their parents. From somewhere in Schlesweg in Germany came news of the birth of two calves which, apparently healthy and well made, had grown as big as their mother within the space of six days and then had reached the proportions of prehistoric animals a month later. Though mild-tempered and docile they could not avoid knocking down houses and stalls, and damaging crops. At Bad Ischl, a spa not far from Vienna, the waters recently had appeared to have acquired the extraordinary power of rejuvenating whoever bathed in them. The skin regained elasticity, marks disappeared, the body became light, vigorous and agile as it had not been since youth. People's memories returned, together with their capacity for work; the flesh also, like a faded rose, reawakened to experience desires it had seemed able to forget forever. A deep and feverish eagerness seemed to animate those bodies, twice young and twice old, as if made greedy by unconscious disbelief in an incubus rather than by full abandonment to ecstasy.

One day, however, the authorities closed the miraculous springs of Bad Ischl. In spite of all precautions and the management's strictest instructions, the staff had allowed the disturbing truth to leak out. The process of rejuvenation had in no case stopped at the age – between twenty and thirty – most yearned for by the spa's elderly clients and, within a few swiftly passing weeks, had so accelerated its backward course that they were finding themselves once more young people, adolescents, children, returning through each age one by one without pause, experiencing anew forgotten tastes and enthusiasms only recalled in some degree by memory. In the final stages of this process in reverse it had become necessary to isolate them, as if to cover a bottomless pit, victims as they were of names and fantasies that appeared as the ghostly figures and senseless shams in a sort of game, though in fact it was the reality of incommunicability suffered during life. In the end it was painful to see these people hidden away in their homes where, looked after by sons and daughters, some were already in their cradles and quite unable to grasp in which age they were living, so many had they traversed as in a dream. Only their eyes remained tired and old, betraying the ever-present memory of their senile years now in bodies of contrastingly childlike form. They appeared trapped by a death disguised as birth; having avoided a natural end at the close of their lives, they had now fallen into death's claws in the act of fleeing from it – that death they now called mamma.

Alarming events were also announced from Russia. But Subotai who governed with extreme severity the surviving population, managed to prevent anything being known, and informed Aiku only when he arrived in Vienna to attend the wedding. He had named it the '1815 syndrome'. More and more frequently news arrived from various parts of Russia about normal people leading ordinary lives except for a fixation common to them all: that of living through one day in the month of June 1815 after the battle of Waterloo. The day might be warmer and rather sultry in the north where arctic nights kept people from their daily rest, breezier and cooler in the east, sunnier and lazier in the south, thundery and more changeable in the west – but in every case a day of that month in that year. By a curious coincidence evidence of that strange aberration had also been noted in the Spanish town of San Sebastian. Many people had been approaching the government to ask why no placards had yet been put up announcing details of bull fights to celebrate King Ferdinand's birthday. For the time of year, according to those good people, was the same as that now current in Russia, June 1815, the month in which festivities were held for the birthday of his catholic majesty Ferdinand VII.

Aiku perceived these varying symptoms as being one and the same evil derangement born of the atom bomb. What conceivable destruction had taken place in the minds of millions of human beings? A jolt had been given to space and time. Not only had the balance of seas, mountains and plants been upset, but so had the conscious awareness of time. What fresh deception had death devised when appearing before its victims? Death was deluding them now, striking them down from afar, as if withdrawing itself into a province never visited before, as if it had not already been there too, in that year 1815, unceasingly endeavouring to even up the numbers between the old and the newborn, to make the sum always seemingly in favour of life. For an instant, touching his chest and legs, Aiku's thoughts pursued the course of that catastrophe without precedent in the memory of man, asking himself what had caused the madness of time, as if seeking reassurance that his own body was young, that his winters, springs, summers and autumns were only thirty-three.

But through his capable hands his body responded healthy and vigorous, telling him to have no fear, not to wander from his path since to him alone time looked for strength to resume the beating of its heart. All those years of wars and conquests, all the earlier ones in the desert at Urga with his father and grandfather, must be in unconscious expectation of a future as extraordinary as only his could be.

"It seems like a disease of the memory, unawareness of the present, fear of living through it, does it not?" asked Marie Christine one day on hearing about the regression to childhood of the old people at Bad Ischl; among them was an uncle of hers, Archduke Rudolph, eighty-five years old, a relative she had never met though he was known in the family as an unrepentant Don Juan. Aiku, knowing what was happening in Russia and in Spain, smiled and nodded. He guessed the secret fear that his young betrothed would not admit, and he could not but love her for this too: might not her maternity be affected by some terrible manifestation? Where in such a world could she bear a healthy child?

"Never fear, Marie Christine, I know there will be a time when you can give birth to our daughter in all tranquillity. The unbalanced state of things will itself give us this certainty." The young Archduchess had always been reassured by Aiku's words since the time she had come to know that in him also was a past that some special power in his nature projected into the future. She had felt touched by his words when, one day before the wedding, looking at the rich gifts sent by the Mongol people, she had whispered to him, "So shall I never see your country?"

"You have already seen it, dear, that evening you were gazing at emptiness in the darkness beyond the garden, just before I asked you to marry me. That was why I chose you, to people that darkness, to put the shades to flight."

In a jubilant Vienna, temporarily forgetful of the cholera, immersed in an atmosphere reviving the magnificent rituals of her past, in the presence of over forty sovereigns in their ceremonial dress ranged in St. Stephen's cathedral, Aiku and Marie Christine appeared before the Pope who, two days earlier, had arrived from Rome.

The previous evening Leo XIV had received a promise from Aiku to have the catholic religion included in the instruction of his children should they wish to be baptised one day. But the two had still not met. Contact between them had been made by cardinals and generals. So this was the first occasion on which they saw each other face to face. Aiku's thoughts returned to Italy and the river on whose banks he had felt that he should halt. The mystery of that day was now becoming clearer though still without an explanation; in his mind he likened it to a piece of shaped iron which, when heated in a furnace, becomes transparent, loses all its features yet is still what it was before. The smile of the vigorous old man brought him new strength, that strength he lacked when his cavalry regiments had stopped at the Po. So there was still time for his conquests, the season of his victories was not yet over. Today it was no longer space but time that could be won. Aiku felt that this old man, who had not been invited to the Vienna Congress, would have been the only worthy interlocutor. Perhaps therefore it had been just as well not to invite him, not to confuse the confines of two sovereignties, thus leaving distinct from one another those of space and time.

The Pope perceived that Aiku desired his blessing. The Tartar leader was not the Antichrist, was not the man his predecessor on his deathbed had thought him to be – of that he felt quite sure. What matter if he did not know Christ? In the ignorance of that barbarian there was a faith, fresher, greater, stronger even than that of Marie Christine, bride from so highly catholic a dynasty as that of the Hapsburgs. God cares not to know the names of His servants; terrible indeed would it have been had not that man appeared to drive the merchants from the temple, to throw down their trading stations. Not even he, the Pope, could have continued his mediation between time and eternity if the space controlled and destroyed by Aiku had not reached the gates of Rome. Aiku no longer had a country, no longer was he a Mongol, just as he himself was, at last, no longer a Lithuanian, anti-Soviet pawn in the Vatican's political calculations. Both of them had finally lost form and identity, belonging to the spirit of the world, pulsating as they merged within it. And to the Pope it seemed the fulfilment of the dream of some great medieval predecessor of his, the generous Utopia of two brothers, a pope and an emperor together ruling the world.

"In verity thou art the High Protector of the world; willingly and with all our heart do we bless thy marriage invoking the protection of Christ!" These words were spoken spontaneously by the Pontiff in Latin. Being unforeseen by ceremonial protocol a tremor of disorientation ran through them all. No need was there to repeat them, however, in the Cathedral of Vienna since the Pope had shouted them aloud, his youthful voice once more restored to him as when, in the baroque Cathedral of Vilnius, he had thundered against the enemies of the faith.

Later, after the lengthy ceremony, the couple received homage at Schönbrunn from all the ambassadors and heads of state present – but before retiring, Aiku wished to visit his faithful cavalrymen of Urga waiting to acclaim him and his bride. Both felt touched when Ude, his lieutenant in Germany, approached to introduce Hilde his future German wife, and asked him, as was their military custom, for permission to marry her.

"Your marriage is a good omen, Ude. You could not have made me a finer present."

Perhaps his own people were beginning to comprehend his dream for a world to be rebuilt. Time permitting, since the space to be conquered was Time.

9

MYSTERIOUS and impossible to hold in check, the '1815 syndrome' was spreading throughout Europe, Asia and Africa – conjuring up ghosts of the plague brought by the Tartars in ancient times. But not everywhere was it the same. At Lhasa in Tibet, for instance, at Jerusalem, the Mecca, Constantinople and at San Jacopo di Campostella, the unknown disease appeared in its most acute form. The local populations seemed to have just woken from a sleep lasting as long as Aiku's wars; they did not know who Aiku was, where he came from and what troubles he had brought. This state of amnesia had begun the day they awoke believing they had dreamed that the saints and divinities revered in their towns had called on them to rebuild their ruined temples. At Delphi, the same loss of memory prevailed: the little Greek town had just then been slowly losing its tourists, its souvenir sellers with their gaily painted carts, its coaches full of noisy foreigners chattering in a babel of languages – even among the ancient stones of the hippodrome along the Sacred Way to the Castalian spring on the slopes of Parnassus – frightening a long snake which many swore they had seen just where Pythia had voiced her replies. Here the land had turned into desert, giving back the sanctuary its original dimensions, as in the days when pilgrims from all over Greece were told to observe silence on entering the olive groves. So the 'umbelicus' of the world, submerged in the soft womb of time, offered the sight that must so have struck the sun-dazzled eyes of Alexander, Caesar and Hadrian as they climbed to the sanctuary of Boeotia to learn their fate from the priests.

It was just then that ambassadors arrived from Imperial Japan. Exceedingly old men, dressed as they would have been at the beginning of the century, they appeared worn out by their long journey. When Aiku received them he realised they had come neither overland nor from the Emperor but, across the provinces of time, had brought from the Emperor's father, the mad Emperor, homage to Franz Josef I, Emperor of Austria and King of Hungary. They had crossed those immense provinces, God alone knew how, like the desert, perilous and unexplored; they had left Tokyo on Saturday July 25th 1914 and had arrived then, nearly a hundred years later. A telephone call to Tokyo could do nothing to clear up the mystery. The lines were down, no one answered, neither ministers, diplomats nor the Imperial Court. The Japanese Ambassador had gone in vain to Vienna airport to meet two of his children returning after a month's holiday in Osaka with their divorced mother. In the last two weeks no planes had arrived either from Japan or from her enormous insular empire extending from Indonesia to Australia. The last train from the Far East had brought news of ships having sailed from Indian and Indo-Chinese ports bound for islands in the Indian and Pacific oceans and which had apparently been swallowed up in fog, having neither received nor transmitted any messages.

Aiku called together all the sovereigns present for the Congress before the most alarming pieces of news could spread further. As soon as the session chaired by Ethelbert opened, the Kings of England and Spain announced that for a month no ships had arrived at the ports of La Coruna and London from the United States nor from any country on the American continent. Neither had any flights from America landed at their airports. The situation over communications with Japan was no different. However amazement turned to consternation when the King of Romania was told that a Portuguese ship had picked up wreckage of a plane flying on the London–New York route, salvaging the black box, from which the King surmised it was the plane taken by his family. The mystery deepened further when the black box revealed that the disaster had been due to lack of fuel, although it was known that proper fuelling had been done at Lisbon. Later they learned that many planes flying to Japan in the last three days had come down in the Bay of Bengal. In every case the reason was the same, lack of fuel, though fuelling had been done only shortly before. The recording of the pilots' voices led them to think that all were greatly concerned at being no longer able to work out flight times, as if the radio and radar at the control towers in countries over which they flew had ceased operating as soon as they had left the last airport in Europe, Asia or Africa.

By now Aiku was beginning to piece together the trend of things. The old continent, and with it the city of his dying grandfather's prophesy, was sinking into its past, adrift in time. Once the moorings holding its decaying countries to the closing century were loosened, no force could keep it back. Aiku could begin the count-down of his reigning years freed from the incubus of being unable to disarm that half of the world he ruled for fear of attack from the other. Slowly everything would return as it had been. He could eliminate aeroplanes, bring back into use slower trains, along with stage-coaches, steam and sailing ships; he could reduce the speed of cars by lowering their horsepower and fuel consumption until the use of horse-drawn vehicles could be restored. He could control the pestilence of television-mania, switch off computers, silence telephones, eliminate rotary presses that deceived the world and deluded it into thinking that information was being provided. Once more he could encourage the art of writing letters that would be received long after they had been written to heighten the flavour and pleasure of distance and absence. Thus could he revive and fortify the languishing sources of wonder and longing as he had tasted them in his own country when, from a mountain top, he had discerned far away the Great Wall of China. The men he had known in his own world, on quitting his charmed and dreamy Mongolia, had become filled up with superfluous information, overcharged with passions entirely strange to them, oppressed by pictures of foreign lands, compelled to learn languages with which their innermost history was at variance, been offered vegetables and meats produced in climates and latitudes more distant than the moon. The bomb, cancer of the world, had arisen from the plague of speed and precision. Massacre rather than murder was the logic of that imbecile world. And the bomb had devoured itself, just as the ogre in the fable, wanting to prove its magic power to the cat, was turned into a mouse and eaten up. Likewise the atom bomb, destroying cosmic balance, had reversed the order of time, stopping the course of centuries, starting to count them backwards, speed killing speed.

Aiku's most disoriented guests at the Congress of Vienna, the American Vice-President and the son of the Emperor of Japan, left, after some weeks of preparation, for the furthest extremities of European and Asian territories, each having decided to wait until the fog – covering that boundless space between them and their countries – had lifted. The American Vice-President set himself up in a villa on the shore of Estoril in Portugal, and people visiting that country, the only neutral one in Europe, went to view from a distance the man who seemed like some precious specimen of an extinct race, always dressed in the same style, in clothes identical to those he had worn in America, often gazing absent-mindedly out to sea muttering to himself as a means of keeping in practice with his own language.

The other great exile, the Prince of Japan, virtual Emperor of an Empire swallowed up by the ocean, was permitted, by grace of the Tsar of All the Russias, to reside on the island of Laragin near the Siberian peninsula of Kamchatka. Having the island at his disposal, as Governor he quickly set up a small court, learning the Kamchatkian language, and soon changing customs, habits, traditions, food, usages – able, like the rest of his people, to absorb the spirit of other worlds. Those who landed on his typically Japanese island found a man more nearly resembling the islanders encountered in that volcanic environment than a member of the Imperial family of Japan. Aiku, who knew what was happening to the two illustrious exiles, felt that two tendencies had become established at the extreme ends of his dominions, in those so widely differing natural surroundings, tendencies always precariously poised in the provinces of time, in the nostalgia of the one and the xenophilia of the other. They seemed to him like the doubled-faced herm of a divinity watching over the equilibrium of the great lands between them – the nought of a circumference that meets the three hundred-and-sixtieth degree. From the inner depths of his empire Aiku awaited a sign of the choices to put into effect. He saw that the process of a return to the past was gaining ground in all regions of Europe, Asia and Africa.

In Europe a tendency prevailed to fix the clock around 1815, with some variations in northern France where most people thought they were living in the latter months of the Directory at the end of the eighteenth century – as though Normandy and Brittany were loath to abandon the last illusions of Republicanism. Russia did not even remember the revolution and the Soviet regime, least of all atomic war and invasion by Aiku's Tartars by now confused with those of Tamerlane. Their days were brightened each morning by the sunshine of the return of Alexander the Blessed, the Tsar who had defeated the French despot and reinstated peace after the terrible wounds inflicted by French occupation. In all churches throughout the Empire the Holy Synod willed that prayers be recited each day by the parish priests for Tsar Alexander I and Tsarina Elizabeth. The Russians unwittingly gained an advantage of forty years of peace by taking refuge in that period of the past, as many years as those that elapsed between 1815 and the Crimean War. The Tsar, only just restored to his throne by the Congress, had been warned by Subotai, his minister in Moscow, that people were expecting to see him in the likeness of the victorious Tsar; there was nothing else to be done except adapt his role to circumstances, and play the part of that great dreamer. In 1815 Poland was looking for a king, first deluded by a hundred promises made by the French Emperor, now by the Corsican's enemies. Aiku had acceded to the Poles' request, certain that this departure from the script of history would not be enough to awaken in them a realisation of their progress backwards and that his gesture would gain him the friendship of that nation too intransigent in its religious fervour to allow for political motives.

In Germany, however, it was hard to understand at what hour in history the clock had been set. Heavily damaged by the bomb he had used to overcome the greatest obstacle in his path after Russia, Aiku felt certain that the imbalance which might well have saved the continent from total collapse had its origins in this country that had been half-destroyed by the bomb considered necessary to overcome it. Sometimes when talking with his wife he had even wondered whether war had broken out between the United States and Japan and whether the two powers, following the natural course of time, still in fact existed after a nuclear conflict. One day at Schönbrunn Marie Christine had brought him the answer to his questions about Germany, showing him a book from the court library.

"Listen, dear. This is the Germany of Tacitus two thousand years ago; but it is Aiku's Germany of today . . . *Adfectatur praecipue asperitas soni et fractum murmur, obiectis ad os scutis, quo plenior et gravior vox repercussu intumescat . . .*" read Marie Christine following the words with her finger and immediately translating them while her husband listened with keen attention. And while she translated Aiku recalled some other words in Latin spoken by the Pope before his departure for Rome, words he had not understood but which had remained imprinted on his mind like so many other mysterious allusions to his destiny: *deposuit potentes de sede et exaltavit humiles . . .*

Yes, it actually was the primitive Germany he had crossed a year earlier, the Germany evoked by his wife, a desolate land where lean and half-savage people wandered among the ruined towns. So, *there* was the most rearward point, the end of the reversal of time from which the world might be able to resume its forward march. From the German traitor Ethelbert he knew that Germany's destiny was to be an emblematic one as though her destructions and rebirths were less total than in the rest of Europe. The destiny of Poliakoff's Russia, though different, was complementary to that of Germany. Russia only achieved victory by submission and several times in her history she had allowed foreign armies to overrun her only to raise herself higher after each fall. There was no limit to the passivity of Russia, the great mother able to take to her breast even her enemies and slowly absorb them in the infinite slowness of her magic time, measured not by output of machines, but by the fruits of each season. In the yielding quality of Russia, the Tartar leader divined that of Asia. The entire continent, whose son he was, looked to him as the real protector from the peril of being compelled to face the realities of today – whether termed economics, military strength, politics or planning of resources. Sleep and flight into the eternal, inclinations instinctive to the mentality of those peoples, were tendencies that, paradoxically, simplified an understanding of whatever the clocks of Asia might indicate. Enough it was to consider only those few peoples who bore the load of national conscience for all the rest who slept the blessed sleep of non-belonging: Iran, Palestine, certain states of India, and the Indo-Chinese peninsula. There, where the pulse of time beat clearer and with greater regularity, men gave signs of having revived the great dream of Islam, of Moslem expansion that had caused medieval Christianity to tremble. Africa had felt this influence, especially north in the Arab countries, but partly too seemed to have resumed the pure and cruel life of a dream in which bloodshed, violence, torture (all the most disordered expressions of greed and force) appeared vain as in a game. Relieved of the terrible suffering implied by conscience and freedom, Africa prolonged her imprisonment of the senses, of her blind force, that lacked expression unless it were implying a secret impulse for death of the individual.

Aiku well knew to what extent those dark urges lived in the mental make-up of his people, now resting victorious in

Europe. In all the strategic decisions taken in recent times, after reaching Italy and the river on whose banks he had called a halt, he had always ensured that the same Tartar troops were never stationed in Africa for more than a month. He himself did not stop there longer than a few hours, to escape the spell woven by that dream; it had happened during a visit to Thebes in Egypt where at sunset the strange sound of the wind blowing off the sandy desert and round the Colossi of Memnon could be heard. The last time he went he had almost fled from it, repressing a temptation to gaze on a city where, as at Delphi, life had stopped, restoring to the ruined temple of Ammon, half suffocated by tall buildings and modern roadways, the dignity of silence and the solitude of an oasis. There he had learned that another victorious warrior, Alexander of Macedon, had come to question the god who spoke through his priests. The god had shown comprehension for the uneasy relationship between a hero and his own father, and had pardoned such acute dissimilarity by revealing himself to be Alexander's real father . . .

For the mosaic of forces under his sway there was a leader, a conscience, but as yet no heir. Aiku keenly felt this need, as did his most faithful followers, preoccupied with that strange future measured by the past. When after closing the Congress of Vienna the sovereigns had finally returned to their own capitals, and the clocks of his dominions had been set at the various ages manifested to their peoples, Marie Christine told her husband that she was expecting a child. At this happy news he immediately went off to tell his officers and therefore the whole world; but then a curious event took place. For the first time for nearly a year the radar stations and machines still left functioning in Europe received signals from the oceans, as if America and Japan were giving momentary proof of their existence. Faint messages in those languages were then heard; finally a plane from Japan landed at London airport. In spite of their somewhat decrepit appearance, the passengers' documents declared their average age to be about forty-five, and they turned out to be members of a great Japanese orchestra, invited two years earlier to play Beethoven's Ninth Symphony at Covent Garden in the presence of the King. After reaching London, however, they barely managed to complete one rehearsal of Schiller's 'Hymn to Joy' when, struck down by a mysterious illness, they all died within the space of a few hours!

Aiku felt that his heir, as yet unborn, had evoked the dream of a world reunited in peace. The time had come, however, when he must devote himself to the birth of his child and to his wife's confinement. In homage to the greatest Queen of England, the country which first had sent its good auspices for his coming, and in memory of his mother born at the southernmost cape of Sakhalin bearing that name, Aiku decided that, should his heir be the longed-for daughter, she would be called Elizabeth.

SECOND
MOVEMENT

M Y PITY for all that is past is that I see; it has been handed over – handed over to the favour, the spirit, the madness of every generation that comes and transforms everything that has been into its own bridge!

A great despot could come, a shrewd devil, who with his favour and disfavour could compel and constrain all that is past, until it became his bridge and prognostic and herald and cock-crow.

This, however, is the other danger and my other pity; he who is of the mob remembers back to his grandfather – with his grandfather, however, time stops.

Thus all that is past is handed over: for the mob could one day become master and all time be drowned in shallow waters.

Friedrich Nietzsche
from 'Of Old and New Law-Tables'
in 'Thus spoke Zarathustra', 11.

translated by R. J. Hollingdale

== 10 ==

THE LAST news received on the old continent about its High Protector was that he and his consort had left for an unknown destination in the Atlantic to await the birth of their heir. Soon, very soon, the '1815 syndrome' got the better of Aiku and swallowed up everything bearing witness to his power and conquests in the complex and tormented political situation that prevailed during that hot summer. Unmindful Europe was an onlooker of the downfall of Napoleon Bonaparte and of his exile to the island of St. Helena; while at Vienna the British, Russian, Prussian and Austrian plenipotentiaries, aided by their allies and by the French minister, put the final, though highly controversial, touches to the map of Europe ravaged by twenty years of war.

Without disturbing the conscience of the Emperor of Austria – by telling him the real story of the men whose prison sentences of varying severity his sovereign was now signing – the Austrian Chancellor had had some dangerous subversives locked up in the fortresses of Ljubljana, Spielberg, Troppau, Verona, Mantua and Peschiera; men of Asian origin caught haranguing the crowd round the Schönbrunn and Hofburg Palaces and trying to enter the Imperial apartments. Declaring they would have nothing to do with that pretence of an Empire, dead and gone nearly two hundred years before, they had affirmed allegiance to the memory of their chief, someone whose short name contained too many vowels – one that a Viennese gentleman thought unfitting to pronounce. Europe, mused the Chancellor, really was in great need of order after all the trouble caused by that French despot and, in his hands, 'Austria Felix' could become an example of how to bring about restoration. The Chancellor disliked revolutionaries of any kind, whether warriors or saints. Visionaries even less, like those mad Mongols or Asians whose folly was probably simulated. At the Emperor's birthday party he had heard privately, from the Hospodar of Moldavia and Wallachia and from the Turkish Ambassador, about news from some provinces, Styria, Galicia, Moldavia, Ottoman Macedonia, concerning Asians who rejected their Emperors and proclaimed fidelity unto martyrdom to their invisible leader.

"Doubtless you would have got rid of the first Christians much better than did Nero," was the acid comment of his daughter when they were alone at table one day, after reading the latest news in the Vienna Gazette giving details about yet another display of her father's inflexible energy. Narrowing her eyes at him, she added, "But are you always so certain of being Clemens von Metternich himself and not a successor who thinks he is him? Maybe actually a Metternich of the same period as those poor Tartars who you say have gone off their heads and cannot find the way home. . ."

This daughter of his first wife, thought the anxious Chancellor, really was a strange woman. All the same there was something unnerving about those men. Their madness had a touch of the heroic spirit, even the least kindly and moderate of his colleagues among the police admitted as much; however he deigned no answer to the remarks of his daughter who maintained her mocking gaze. But no one governing so complex a pattern of races and religions could take notice of some mere singularity, not even – as he had read in the report on the questioning of one of those madmen at Debrecen – hearing it affirmed that their chief had married the Emperor of Austria's daughter and that the Pope himself had actually blessed the union!

Even less could one such as he waver before a question of doubtful identity. Certainly the most extraordinary things had happened in recent years. People were still at sixes and sevens on account of the speed of so much disaster and ruin, wars and massacres. What had occurred during the last twenty years in Europe was no mere figment of the imagination and perhaps many had sought in madness an ultimate salvation, especially following the Russian campaign. Rather like those insane people, he too had bowed to circumstances seeking to save his country by arranging a marriage between one of his Emperor's daughters and the adventurer who had brought Europe to her knees. Thinking over that shameful affair which he had done so much to further, he still felt a wave of indignation. The Emperor's daughter and that savage. . . What misdeeds had been committed! All those shocks had been too deeply felt. He had heard from the Department of Health that throughout the Empire there had been a strange increase in the numbers of those admitted to psychiatric hospitals. The Chancellor of Saxony, Baron von Andergast, had told him in confidence that in Germany there had never been so many cases of insanity – though the proper scientific term was schizophrenia – as there had been in only a few months of that year, 1815. "Especially so since 'he' had taken himself off, thank heavens," the corpulent Chancellor had sighed.

The odd thing was that, like a sort of infection, hallucinations of a similar kind had appeared here and there among people who, insane of course, declared they were living in 1998. Doctors had coined an expression to name this form of mental disturbance, seemingly imported from the Far East because so many Asians were affected, calling it the '1998 syndrome'.

What troubled years they were, so many traditions lost, truths denied, pernicious ideas rooted in young minds, distortions to correct in every area: religion, education, universities, academies. Neither had the Holy Spirit been of much aid to the Church, promoting to the threshold of Peter that poor fellow of a Barnabas Chiaramonti, Pius VII, – a saint for many believers, though personally he felt he would have cut a better figure as priest of some parish in central Italy. "States are not governed by reciting the Lord's Prayer," as one of their most trusted allies, the Grand Duke of Tuscany, cousin of his Emperor, had sagely said to him in Italian one day when they were discussing the Concordat which had permitted the Vatican, after protracted negotiations, to grant so many privileges to the despot of Europe.

As the Chancellor of Saxony had said, in confidence to his Austrian opposite number, mental health in Germany had never been at such a low ebb. Neither Luther's doctrine, nor the legend of Faust, nor the witches of the night of Valpurga, had made such a deep impression on the collective psyche as had the invading armies of that demon from nowhere. From Darmstadt, Heidelberg, Würsburg, Köln and Baden reports were arriving of strange hallucinations impossible to separate from the '1998 syndrome'. Men and women woke in the middle of the night crying out in terror that the house was burning with a fire as terrible as that which had destroyed Sodom and Gomorrah, sent down from heaven by 'him'. Even children, who knew nothing of the despot, on waking succumbed to fright and tried to save their animals and dearest possessions; all this as if it had nothing to do with a battle which, though fearful, was at least fought at a distance, but rather with a lethal and invisible miasma spreading through the air. The luminaries of the Berlin Royal Faculty of Medicine believed that the destruction and suffering of the people in Prussia and in the other states had led to that mental disease which had turned the great national enemy into a kind of Attila or primordial force for evil – the wolf in the Grimm brothers' fable.

"Phenomena already noted when the Tartars invaded Eastern Europe and the Turks roamed the Mediterranean. . . Mass hallucinations that slowly disappear," announced the men of science, and shook their heads. And they ordered cold baths and floggings to be doubled for those whose infectious folly seemed the most dangerous, while an increasingly generous number of straight-jackets and restraining beds were made ready.

Only Russia somewhat resembled Germany in her collective psychosis, though the arrival in Moscow of the charismatic Tsar Alexander from Vienna aroused such wild enthusiasm as to diminish the phenomenon in all the provinces where the invading armies had left such terrible marks of their passage. No one, however, could have foreseen that the very man who had defeated the invader and represented for all his people the best assurance that the incubus was over, would himself fall victim to this collective delusional condition.

"Were I certain you would never mention this matter to a living soul, I would confide in you something that would amaze you as much as it worries me," said the Russian sovereign's first Gentleman-in-waiting one day to the Archduke Ranier of Hapsburg in the Belvedere Palace, when on a visit to Vienna for the marriage of his daughter to an Austrian nobleman. The two had met during the Congress of Vienna and their mutual passion for women had led them both to frequent theatres and cabarets; they had thus become close friends and spent time together whenever the opportunity arose.

"Tell me, dear friend; I shall be silent as the grave," replied the Archduke in an encouragingly low voice, drawing up his chair. His glance of circumspection round the room seemed entirely unnecessary, coffee having been served and the Archduchess having withdrawn.

"Our Tsar is showing clear signs of insanity. He has a fixed idea of having been called to the throne by the Congress summoned in Vienna by 'him'. He says he used to live in Tuscany, bred horses and was married to an Italian countess; he weeps and moans at night fearing 'he' will return."

The Archduke who had been hoping for some amusing complication in his friend's gallant adventures, though a little disappointed, promptly pretended interest. "But what do you mean? Does he really believe 'he' will escape from St. Helena?"

"No, I'm not talking about that island. . . He says 'he' will come back with his Austrian wife and his daughter but that no one knows when or where from."

"My poor friend, I now appreciate your concern. . . though from what you have told me on other occasions, your sovereign has always been a little, well, excitable, easily upset, a great and wonderful dreamer. . ."

"But never like he is now. It must be all the stress and strain of the patriotic war, so long drawn out. You never saw him during the nights when 'he' held Council meetings in the Kremlin and sent messengers to bring back his surrender. Then he really did seem about to lose his mind."

"I would hardly say, though, that it seems a dangerous madness," returned the Austrian more out of curiosity to know the rest than to reassure his friend.

"For days he has not received any of his ministers. I myself, his first Gentleman-in-waiting, don't see him. He has shut himself up alone in his palace at Tsarkoie Selò and refuses to see anyone. He is contemplating making a long journey to visit our most important monasteries and consult our most revered *staretz.*"

"Oh well; he always was rather a mystic. . ." Ranier of Hapsburg concluded the conversation slapping his friend on the shoulder. He would have given the matter no further thought had not an incident occurred just a week later which brought it back to mind.

He had been obliged to go to Moravia to inspect an artillery practice. The journey was long, and he had just arrived in his carriage at the Governor's palace in Brno when a noise of carts and voices shouting orders filled the air of that quiet little town, caught his attention and brought him out onto his balcony. From there he saw a column of political prisoners being taken to the fortress of Spielberg, the grim building set on a hill directly opposite. One thing struck him particularly; all the prisoners were Chinese and Asians, some definitely Mongols judging by the shape of their eyes and of their heads. He felt curious to go and ask the major leading the column what it was all about. So many Asian prisoners, he thought; whatever could they have to do with the Austrian Empire?

One of the prisoners, a severe, intelligent-looking man, saw him talking with the major and, tugging hard at the companion chained to him, approached near enough to address Ranier. "Just think that our leader put even the Tsar of Russia on the throne, that imposter who was breeding horses in Italy! And now, we're here, powerless, in chains and no one believes us, not even many of our brothers who have lost their reason. . ."

Dropping his whip, Ranier turned sharply and stared at the Mongol, motioning the soldiers on guard to let him speak. It was true; on his journey he had caught sight of many Asians doing heavy work, more than he had ever seen in the past. And his allusion to the Tsar, how could it be?

"Who is. . . your leader?"

"One from our parts. He'll be back here one day with his wife and daughter, but none of us know when. You see, Sir, the bomb has reversed the order of time, people think we are in 1815 but they're wrong. . . The Tsar knows perfectly well what year it is, Metternich too and also your Emperor. You too, if you try and remember, if you shut your eyes. . ."

Ranier lowered his gaze before the Mongol, who was studying him narrowly. Things swam before him, a pain shot through his head; he felt dazed by a nauseous smell. Though momentary, that smell was unmistakable. He had not thought of it since the time he had kept watch by his mother's dead body in the chapel of Belvedere that hot summer when she died. It was the same smell.

As if reading his thoughts the Mongol spoke, "Many are the living and the dead, and you have smelled it. . . Like the old people at Bad Ischl spa who have returned to youth. . ."

Ranier made as if to clutch the arm of a guard. He felt he saw a white room full of cupboards and desks covered with papers and, on his desk, a grey object with a black thread that rang at regular intervals. And on the desk there was also a shiny metal nameplate with his name engraved on it in italics.

With an effort he came to and immediately reassured the major and officers who had approached to help him in what seemed a fainting fit.

"It is nothing, gentlemen, thank you, really nothing at all. . . the journey, the heat tired me, that is all."

"Of course! It's a leap, Sir, not a journey, from 1998 back to 1815. A dangerous leap. . ." shouted the prisoner like one obsessed, as they dragged him off and the column was ordered to proceed on its way.

In the following days although Archduke Ranier of Hapsburg, a healthy thirty-year old, married to a cousin of the Hungarian branch of the family, carried on inspecting the artillery practice as best he could, he felt unwell, though continuing to blame the heat and his tiring journey. He had a curious sensation of being in some other place; on leaving a room the floor seemed to move as if walls, windows, chandeliers were settling back in place after a brief earth tremor. Yet there had been no tremor. If he gazed at the horizon for too long, at the gently sloping hills in that part of Moravia, he invariably seemed to see blue smoke and, through it, vague forms of people and houses, men moving fast on vehicles without horses, tall houses full of windows, like towers but wider, set in rows.

Then a day came when during a report he was giving to the officers, he felt their chilly bewildered looks turned upon him; he hardly dared to ask the reason but, realising he must, forced himself to speak. The captain of the battery however forestalled him.

"Your Highness was speaking in an almost incomprehensible language; such a strange German. . ."

That day he decided to break off his inspection work and telegraphed to Vienna for an urgent medical examination. He must get treatment, he was really ill.

The night after this decision he could not rid his mind of the thought of Tsar Alexander, weeping and fearful of 'his' return. But who was 'he'? How could that Mongol have known what terrors were besetting the Tsar? Clearly 'he' was not the man on St. Helena, so who was he? Why had the prisoner said he had jumped nearly two centuries and was tired because of it? What was the meaning of those shapes he saw in the distance, of the language he had used when speaking to the officers? And the sensation of being somewhere different from where he knew himself to be?

He was up at dawn having had no sleep all night. He ordered the carriage to be prepared. Before returning to Vienna he wanted to go to the fortress of Spielberg.

When the Archduke Ranier appeared, the Tyrolean gentleman in command of the fortress could not refuse the singular request to speak with a prisoner, though it greatly embarrassed him. Definitive orders regarding treatment of the group of Chinese and Mongols had not yet arrived from Vienna but he guessed they were to be very strictly segregated. All the authorities had to do was decide whether to classify them as subversives or as political prisoners: it depended if they had been allowed to benefit from being considered semi-insane, but he knew they would be regarded as subversive and no excuse of illness would be accepted. It was strange though that a member of the Imperial family should take an interest in one of them, worrying too that he looked so pale and feverish. He had never before seen the young Archduke, though he had heard him mentioned in connection with the recent artillery practice. In any case there was no time to send for advice from the Governor of Moravia, and there was no reason for suspicion. If you could not trust a Hapsburg who, in that Empire, could you trust?

There was one rather absurd detail however; the Archduke did not know the prisoner's name. They could not all be paraded together for recognition, it was too dangerous and rules forbade this to be done on any account. There was nothing for it but to show them to him through the peepholes in the cell doors. They climbed the Tower of the Scorpion where the prisoners were held, and Ranier easily recognised the one who had so upset him. It had been hard to hide from the Governor his uneasiness and the malaise he felt at the sight of those prisoners in their cells. So defenceless yet so dignified, they had an aura of natural superiority as if it were they who agreed to be shut in – even though not for long, almost as if they were awaiting him, as if his coming explained their detention. They spoke no word but their haunted eyes shone with emotion as if reproaching him for a cowardly action which he knew he had committed.

"Why go on pretending not to understand? Why are you so contemptible?" some of them seemed to say. Once more giddiness overcame him, obliging him to lean against the wall, his eyes half-closed.

"Highness, are you ill? We can go outside if this air is bad for you," said the Governor hurriedly, pleased if he could end that worrying visit and beginning to feel he had had enough of the Archduke.

"I have already told him, it is not the air nor his journey that makes him feel ill. He has made a leap of nearly two hundred years but he won't believe me," the unmistakable voice of that same man reached him. He asked them to open the heavy iron door and let him stay locked in with the prisoner so as to talk with him alone.

"I will call you, do not fear," said Ranier to the puzzled Governor who had no choice but to obey. Prudently, however, he hid two guards behind pillars in the corridor.

When Ranier and the Mongol prisoner were face to face in the dim light from the barred window further screened by three layers of iron netting, they remained in silence

110

for a few minutes. Emotion on both sides was too strong and both felt the absolute need of understanding each other.

Before Ranier stood Zeja, one of Aiku's closest collaborators, the man who had subdued all the eastern part of Aiku's dominions, conquering Asia from India to Palestine. Zeja had pressed the switch releasing the bomb on Russia when Aiku gave the order. He had realised at once that the young aristocrat must belong to the family Aiku had put back on the Austrian throne, a member of which he had married. And if he was now standing there wearing that suffering and agitated expression, it meant that the words he had spontaneously uttered at their first meeting had shaken one area of the young man's mind, uncertain between past and future. But even if Zeja could make him understand the truth, what advantage could he, in chains, gain for the man unless it were a reputation of being insane? The whole thing had become so absurd that no one would ever be able to help free them from their hopeless situation, witnesses of a truth that could not be told. And yet, standing before him was that Hapsburg who believed himself an inspector of the Empire's artillery, holding rank of major general, not just some decorative bank official, as were so many of the family. Zeja thought he should attempt to open the man's mind even if it meant risking his sanity. There must be a thread with which to unravel that tangled skein, there somewhere must be the corner-stone of that bedevilled castle that would give way to that month of June, so hot and oppressive. . . Aiku would one day return, he was not dead.

"Why have you come?" asked Zeja brusquely, stroking his white beard which was still veined with black.

"Because you know there is something I want to understand. I cannot stay long. The Governor is suspicious. Perhaps

I can be useful to you in some way, but speak, tell me where the truth lies."

"The truth? The truth lies today in the gloom of fortresses, in the horror of lunatic asylums. In all Europe the only ones who know it today are the subversive and the insane."

"What do you mean?"

"I'm telling you, these are times of calamity for Europe unless 'he' returns."

"No easy matter from St. Helena; but why do you think he could save Europe if he returned? Already he has needlessly shed much blood in his thirst for power."

"Him thirsty for power? He came to create a world like the one in his own country. You are trying to learn from me who you were, or rather who you will be, but it is not having met me that made you wonder. Your present sickens you, it is the nausea you will feel at work, at your desk, on the telephone, while you listen to the world by radio and you are shut in, there in your box. Most of you are not in the same place as where your bodies are. . . If you could only see yourselves in the holy confusion born of your unhappiness! No one would recognise themselves again. . ."

"But who is 'he'?"

"I am no longer sure I know it myself, who he was, who he will be. We were born in the same land, I lived close to him for years, we fought together in the mountains of our country, then away to conquer the world. And now, together, we have lost our freedom. What you see is not the world we won."

"I well believe you. I too see another distant one. So I came to ask you to explain, to save me from losing my reason like the poor Tsar of Russia."

"He's not mad at all."

"And who am I, then?"

"I cannot tell you. I am not sure I know, even though I must have met you before. Are you not a Hapsburg?"

"Oh yes, I am an Archduke right enough." Ranier sighed with relief.

"But which? I shall meet so many flocking round 'him', young like you; some of their names will embellish various financial institutions. . ."

"My name is Ranier, if that means anything to you. Does it?"

"Perhaps it does. . . But hold on to your uncertainty; it's a valuable asset. Don't believe in the omnipotent present as they, the 'sane', are doing. This age is in fact already past, dead; if we can keep the secret we shall one day rid ourselves of the fear of never really knowing who we are, of being unable to inhabit one single moment, past, present and future."

"How can I make that man outside come and open the door, let me return to my place in the world as if nothing had happened? You have opened wounds that go too deep for me."

"On the contrary, I have helped you to recover. Soon they will believe you insane or will arrest you as they have us; thus will you be saved. But if you really want proof of what I have said, go to the Capuchin Crypt in Vienna where your family lies. There, on the tombs underground, if not already barred to the living, you will see the real truth behind fortresses and mental hospitals."

Ranier wanted to put a stop to it all. He had heard enough. In hurried tones he called the guard to open the door.

"If you take my advice, you will stay here, find some excuse, or say you're ill, but stay, learn to remain within yourself. There is already the whole world. Do not be deceived by the dates out there, by the call of the flesh, by the strength of your loins, do not breed children, do not you too sow the seed

113

of death. Out there you will no longer be a man like other men. The truth you have learned in this prison will never be forgotten, never more will you be able to re-enter your time."

But Ranier was beating harder on the heavy door, closed by three turns of the key; would he never be able to open the door of time, never be safe? He stopped his ears to avoid hearing Zeja's words that drove deeper and deeper into his soul. Guns firing a single shot from a redoubt in the fortress brought back to him a sense of normality: so it must be mid-day. But what was holding up that cursed guard? Why did he not come and open, what were they doing out there? Above all why had he ever come to the castle. . .? In all that horror one thought alone sustained him: the pregnant wife he had left in Trieste. He would go to her at once; he would deceive her no more. Thenceforth he would live for her and the child. Never had the thought of becoming a father so comforted him as in that moment. A child, yes, an anchor tying his existence to a blind biological purpose, to a date, a time, his time. Surrender to his own death redeemed by fatherhood.

The fears aroused by the Mongol's words still froze his bones, restoring the full sweetness of desires he had never valued in their entirety, the beauty of Nature's deceits which in his profligate life he had always derisively eluded. At last the heavy door swung slowly, creaking on its hinges. The purple face of the Governor with his guards, guns pointed, filled the opening. Storming past them Ranier rejected offers of an escort as far as Brno. Outside he jumped into his carriage and looked neither back nor through the window till darkness fell as they were nearing Prague.

In Prague he wished to stop no longer than strictly necessary to change horses, and pressed so hard for haste that, although honoured by the presence of an Archduke, the people there

114

showed some irritation. After twenty-four hours of headlong driving, the towers and spires of Vienna could be seen from the hills of Grinzing. Ranier was fighting a temptation which had been racking him for many hours, growing as they neared the capital. Earlier during his journey he had felt sure he would not give way to it, but now he knew where his carriage would go first – to the Capuchin church. The coachman Franz heard his master shout the order; alright, did he think his servant was deaf? On reaching the church the Archduke leapt out of the carriage, catching his cloak in the hinges of the door and tearing it. As it was nine o'clock at night the monastery's portal was closed but, on hearing who knocked, the holy father on duty immediately welcomed him and requested him to wait. There was a rule that members of the Imperial family must be received by the Prior. Half-an-hour later he appeared and, with the deference accorded to the Hapsburgs, asked the reason for the visit so that he could best satisfy his Highness's wishes.

What answer could he give this venerable man? That he wanted to see with his own eyes if his tomb were already lined up with the others in the crypt – not far from those of Karl VI, Marie Thérèse and Franz Stefan? He thought up the pretext that he was conducting some important piece of historical research on the great eighteenth-century Empress, and needed to know the exact dates of birth of two of her daughters, buried there with their mother. A futile reason, especially at that hour, the Prior's severe expression seemed to say; but he made no comment except a slight nod of the head. It would not do to say no to a Hapsburg and the Prior, requesting the guard to bring the keys, prepared to accompany the Archduke. In silence they descended some flights of stairs. At every other step the Prior's pale sandal-shod feet appeared from below his dark habit. The light dimmed, recalling to Ranier those dolorous scenes during the funeral of his mother who had died when he was only eight, and had been buried after two nights in the mortuary chapel. Those broad black stones, the curving stairway, the torches flickering on the walls, like those in the fortress of Spielburg, had many times peopled his nightmarish dreams. He had never been there again, not in all those twenty-two years. Though his position had obliged him to attend the funerals of his illustrious relations, he had never ventured beyond the threshold of the crypt. At the bottom the Prior with some difficulty opened the door leading into the underground vaults where lay those famous guests of the Capuchin church. How many doors such as this had slowly opened before him lately. . . which would be the next one? A heavy sweetish odour filled the air, a mixture of spices and melted candle wax, stuffiness and age-old damp. There, underneath, lay his mother. . . or was he himself underneath?

"Here we are, your Highness. If you will be good enough to follow me, I will lead you to where Marie Thérèse lies. Her children are buried in a circle round her, all except Marie Antoinette of France who, as your Imperial Highness well knows, was unable to reach her mother. . . On the tomb you will find something about her daughters – of whose dates of death you seem in some doubt."

"Thank you Father, we will go now." How difficult it was to continue peering at the tombs, there was such a poor light and he did not want to arouse the friar's suspicions further.

But there was no longer anyone else in the crypt, as he immediately realised. He searched to right and left, in the corridors where the heavy greenish-bronze sarcofagi were lined up, divided into groups. The torches on the walls threw only his own shadow, unlikely evidence of his existence. The friar could not possibly have disappeared; where was he? At that moment he heard the door close. The friar had gone and had left him alone. A few steps away, on his right, he saw the baroque bronze tomb of his mother and, next to it, in the same style, another only slightly less corroded and not so old. Bending, he read on it a Ranier of Hapsburg's date of death.

11

H E WOULD never return alive, that was certain. From St. Helena there was no escape. For fifteen years their lives had been united by unbreakable ties. Today he felt an emptiness as if that flash of lightning had torn off a strip of flesh, as if he knew the wound would never heal in all the days left to him. Death seemed closer to the Pope now that the great enemy of his life had been subdued. At times, recalling memories of the past, sharper in the early hours after that final downfall, he even felt some slight affection for the enemy he had known. The game of history has its own rules, one being that a great victor needs a great loser by his side, as had happened with other popes, with other chiefs and leaders.

And supposing he were to return? Even only for a few months, and give another fright to those who had prevailed at the Congress of Vienna. . . To make them aware yet again of their own ineptitude, bring home to them the fact that only a common fear of seeing him race across Europe once more at the head of his armies legitimised their unity. . . To humiliate the pride of that Metternich who, while protesting his son's devotion, failed to respect the interests of the Church and, after crossing the Po, had invaded Ferrara and Comacchio, cities for centuries under papal rule. . . To the Pope it seemed as if he had already lived through the best years of his life and pontificate. The memory of that genius would certainly tail behind that of his most illustrious victim. Yet he had believed him, had been sincerely convinced. In spite of opposition from so many cardinals, that day he had gone to his capital so far from Rome to bless, before all those defeated sovereigns, the power he held. That most singular man had never crossed the Po, had never entered Rome as if held back by respect for some invisible prohibition. . .

Himself a victim of the same universal malady, Leo XIV relived, in his own life, that of the long-dead Pius VII. The Lithuanian, son of a miner, now believed himself the Italian Pope, descendant of a princely family of Cesena, whose mother, dying in a convent in an atmosphere of sanctity, had foreseen that her son, successor to the prince of Apostles, would undergo the most severe trials in the history of the Church. But even more: by a curious process of symbiosis his physical appearance seemed slightly altered, thinner and somewhat bent, as Pius VII appeared in the ascetic portraits made of him towards the close of his life. Now seated in his study lost in thought, shortly after the private mass held in the chapel of the palace, he awaited his daily cup of chocolate for breakfast brought him by his oldest retainer, Carlino, already decrepit and deaf.

"Those wretches; there's no getting rid of them. The dirt they make, and always coming back to this window!"

Carlino often talked to himself and, slowly sinking into the solitude of deafness, had taken to recalling people and events of seventy or eighty years ago; the Pope hardly took notice any more of what he said.

119

"Your Holiness, breakfast is ready," but having laid down the silver tray on the table, Carlino immediately returned to the window and resumed his anxious chatter. The Pope wondered what had happened to upset him so much that morning. Perhaps it was that rustling sound he too had heard just lately. But if his servant was deaf? Now that he thought of it, he had heard that noise at night as well, from the bedroom that opened onto his study. But Carlino went on grumbling. . .

"What has happened to upset you like this?"

"Your Holiness, we cannot let those birds make their nest right on your windowsill! Be off. Right up against the Holy Father's window they had to come and nest, these. . .

The Pope had taken a sip of chocolate; too hot. Carlino really was not himself that morning. Getting up he approached the open window. A pair of beautiful birds, blue, pink-streaked feathers on their necks, with red wings and brown bodies, observed him. Evidently they were not born at the latitude of Rome. Underneath the hen there seemed to be a type of nest, wisps of straw mixed with mud that somehow the cock had found nearby. So it was they he heard moving about at the window during the night. And they seemed entirely unafraid, less so of his white figure than of anything else. Where could they have come from?

"Carlino, leave them alone. The hen is nesting, you should be ashamed of disturbing her. Bring them some food, go to the gardener."

"Your Holiness, I obey and will go, but you will hardly let them lay eggs on your windowsill?"

"And why not, poor things. . . But perhaps it would be best for them to nest somewhere safer. A Pope's house changes hands so often, his keys quickly pass from one hand to another. . ."

120

Gently the Pope made as if to stroke the hen. What marvellous colours; where could they be from? he wondered. The cock seemed to want to come nearer, and moved close to the Pope who stretched out his hand to bless the two creatures – as in Giotto's fresco showing birds talking and listening to the Saint of Assisi. If he too could speak to them, send them – not into space, a prison where one like himself felt the perpetual inadequacy of men and their society – but upwards, up into time, beyond that June of 1815 when, in the confrontation between a weary pope and an imprisoned emperor, the conflicting concepts of eternity and time wasted to nothing. Were those two creatures to fly up to the throne of God and say to him that mankind was unworthy of being saved and pardoned, that it knew neither love nor hate nor could it oppose his holy religion with a potent and diabolical pride; that still the only one to have possessed a trace of such virtues was far away, bound to an Atlantic rock, a new Prometheus in chains. . .

"Great God, give Thy animals the grace offered in vain to man, let a new order arise through Thy avenging justice! Let a divine and inhuman force impose a great silence in words spoken on earth and let these Thy creatures begin a new cycle of the cosmos freed from the time of our ambiguous uncertainty. Time was Thy curse laid upon us for our sin in having aspired to Thy likeness, Thou who art mirrored in none. . . Time is a prison from which no one escapes unless by death, the mystery to which Thou hast made glory and beauty surrender, gifts which more than all others suffer outrage. No glory deceives these creatures, neither doth beauty make them vain; unknown to them are the torments to which men deliver themselves up, when it is Thy will in conferring upon them these gifts that they should be freed. Give us this day the death brought by our intelligence, the grace to renounce reason and

121

to embrace the folly of the saints, the idiots, the persecuted in all the darkest of our fortresses and prisons at this hour! If in my hour on earth I have done some deed worthy of Thy grace, oh Lord, it was in the prison of him who is now overthrown, when life flowed by, irresponsible, justified in days one like another, far from this city of Rome where two thousand years have been spent solely in widening the abyss between Thyself and man, oh Lord. . . Perhaps only then was I the nameless 'pope' who heard the birds that alighted at the window of my house as at that of any other."

Just as the Pontiff concluded his prayer the birds commenced singing under his joyful gaze. As they sang, Castor and Pollux in the group of marble statues in the centre of the square appeared more undecided than ever whether to choose consciousness or sleep, condemned as they were to spend six months in life and six in death.

When the Pope went to bed that night and sleep at last came to him, the birds of paradise haunted his dreams. They appeared as a precious gift from the Queen of England, wife of King Charles I, to the Pope of Rome in 1639. There had been a lively argument between the Queen and the King over the latter's unwillingness to send a ship as far as the Antilles to procure a pair of birds of paradise. In his dream the Pope, knowing of the tragedy that would soon befall the King (that is, of having his head removed), wished to intervene, assuming the material form of one who endeavoured to persuade the Queen how dangerous such a gesture of homage to the Church would be. One image succeeded another, nurtured by his own anxieties:

"Whatever kind of a King are you if you cannot even send one of your ships to fulfil your Queen's desires?"

"A whim, Henrietta, a mere whim; they will say it was an arbitrary decision of the Crown. I can almost hear the

Roundheads croaking. . . Could you not make do with a pair of peregrine falcons, or larks, or sparrow-hawks, or cormorants. . . some bird from my kingdom, I mean, for your gift to the Holy Father?"

"Mon cher, in the Pope's garden they will protect us," replied Henrietta evading his question, "when he strokes them he will think of us, if we are no longer here."

In his dream the Pope felt a weakening of resistance in the Stuart King who was to show such strength facing death by execution. In love with his wife, he assented to her request and a ship of the British Navy, manned by a crew faithful to the royal house, sailed from Plymouth. The Pope dreamed that the ship took exactly one year to reach its destination, find a pair of birds of paradise, capture them and take the homeward road. The Captain, a young nobleman, was in his cabin writing up the journal when a sudden uproar made him hasten out on deck. There was much excitement among the crew, and voices shouted that England had been sighted. Yes, that dark mass was the tip of Cornwall just visible, a day's sailing distance away. The Pope felt that the young Captain was quite as moved as were all the seamen at the thought of home, wondering if things were still the same after that year-long voyage. There came a shout from the look-out: to starboard a schooner was drifting on the current with no one on board.

When they drew nearer, however, a few feebly moving men crawled into view – all that was left of a company of Irish soldiers, faithful to the King, who had fled from London a month before, while the rest had been annihilated by Cromwell's army. Their horrible tale was barely comprehensible: the King beheaded, the Queen exiled in France, a Republic proclaimed with Oliver Cromwell as Lord Protector. Thousands of Englishmen had died, much property had been confiscated. The Captain's father had been one of the first to be executed in the Tower of London. Those poor men urged him to go no farther, to seek another place at which to land. England was no longer England!

The Pope then saw the Captain give the order to turn away and the ship began its desperate aimless wandering. At last one day, tired of roaming the ocean, having had to seek supplies and water at islands most distant from British routes, both crew and Captain decided to pass the Straits of Gibraltar and resolved to end their life as fugitives. Once in the land-bound sea the ship was finally intercepted, fired on and taken – but the English of Cromwell's Republic found no one alive on board. Only a short distance away, in the sky, the Pope seemed to see the pair of splendidly coloured birds flying from the ship towards the coast of Italy, across the Pontine marshes in the direction of Rome. Those birds of paradise flying up to him through time as his prayer would have wished, ascending in a world without end before the throne of God. . .

12

NO ONE ON the island in the Atlantic to which the High Protector and his Consort had withdrawn could have counted the years since their arrival. How many had passed or how many had turned back in reverse? There, no one worried about the '1815 syndrome', as if the course of time had been freed from the chains of a succession only in one direction. Occasionally Aiku thought that time was settling down, resembling the point of a balance swinging before stopping on the number assigned. The only certain thing was the number of his eight beautiful children, three girls and five boys, whose births had marked at intervals the period of exile. Aiku could not tell if they had been created to put off any return, or if the impossibility of return had led to their creation. His days on the island were almost entirely devoted to their education; everyone in the High Protector's little court seemed to consider this their main object in life: to look after those children and bring them up to an age when an evil spell would be dissolved and the gateway to return would re-open. Then Elizabeth, Aiku's cherished and long-desired firstborn, would be able to reign over a renewed world, cured of the sickness of time.

"This place resembles Purgatory. . . At the end of the world it will exist no more, there will only be Paradise or Hell," said Marie Christine one evening, as if talking to herself, looking out in the twilight over the ocean from the highest terrace in the house. Aiku who was less well versed than she in the Christian religion and its Four Last Things – Death, Judgement, Hell, Heaven – did not trouble to ask what his wife meant. But looking out from the terrace with her, he felt that the hour of sunset enhanced the most intimate fascination of that place, neither shaded nor light, different from his Mongolia where, at the springs of the Onon river in his own region, evening light gave way to darkness so suddenly that one hardly noticed when it happened, as if light and darkness only could exist, one giving no quarter to the other.

The view over the ocean never failed to charm him, recalling the day when they had arrived from across those waters on board the British cruiser *Cardiff* commanded by Admiral Maitland; his left hand was missing, yet he nevertheless seemed to talk more with his 'hands' than with his mouth, as if the missing one evoked the time of its loss. They had set out from an Istrian port near Trieste where the ruins of a splendid abbey could still be seen. At the sight of them Marie Christine had shivered and pointed them out to her husband.

"After it was rebuilt a young couple lived in it for many years – ancestors of mine, an Archduke who left for Mexico to take power there. He returned a corpse from over that ocean, having been deposed and shot. A wretched omen for us that we should sail from here. . ."

"But I am not of your family, no one of mine ever left those ruins. Do not fret."

The ship was the last to leave Istria in their age. Behind

her, as if her wake enclosed and swallowed up all shipping routes and navigation marks, days passed without their sighting anything except the odd Spanish galleon and a few sailing boats: British and French sailing ships, more British than French, but fewer and fewer motor-driven ships until eventually no more were seen – no smoke stacks, no sirens. Aboard the *Cardiff*, where the radar and all sophisticated equipment was out of order, there was enough fuel only for a limited number of knots, barely sufficient for reaching that island after passing Gibraltar.

"We cannot go back, dear, we have no more fuel. Aren't you glad?" Having descended from the gangway Aiku smiled and offered his arm to Marie Christine.

"Is it some game or a nightmare? It does not seem right for living people to see this mountain, this island. I'm afraid, Aiku. Do something so that we can go back. Please do," murmured Marie Christine holding him close.

"But surely not? There is no better place for our daughter. No one knows who we are; it is like landing somewhere left out of all maps by mistake. No one will find us here unless we want them to. Not even Death!"

Aiku was enthusiastic. During those first days after their arrival, when his followers had to be settled into the most comfortable hotel on the island, he was tireless and cheerful. With the local authorities – who seemed regretful at being unable to offer a more sumptuous welcome – he had the impression of arousing a kind of admiration, one albeit tinged with awe and compassion, as if a tragic destiny, stronger than any will, had led him to land on those shores. A few days after they had come, the Governor of the island was the first to reveal how calamitous was the period of history which had witnessed entry of the majestic cruiser *Cardiff* into their narrow port.

127

"Had I not seen that ship with my own eyes, I would never have believed that Metternich would allow his Emperor's daughter to board her too!"

Aiku kept silent, waiting with an ambiguous smile. Though a painful task, the Governor felt he must talk to him and face the most disagreeable part of his duty in the matter.

"We are still awaiting instructions from Vienna, but your majesty can count on my sense of honour. We shall never be the gaolers of the greatest man of our time."

In their room that evening Aiku and Marie Christine decided they would never give any reply to the strange comments of the local people; of the same opinion were the members of their suite who had already noted the inconsistency of certain questions and the embarrassed air of those who asked them. It was also agreed that his followers would answer to the new French surnames of Gourgaud, Montholon, Bertrand – the ones which had been used in addressing them.

"For us this island has no name, it has no part in our recollections; if it has a name for them that is enough. I do not know to what authority, kingdom or republic they belong. However, let us all try to show respect for this state, perhaps the king is a friend of one of those summoned to Vienna."

In the early days there was no trouble over observing this rule. The Governor's guards on duty at the hotel kept a discreet distance and might have been taken for bodyguards or sentries. This discretion prevented members of the party from knowing whether they were guests or prisoners. Problems soon arose however when Count Huniady, the High Protector's Secretary, explained clearly to his master that their stock of money, the Austrian crowns taken from a bank before they departed, was running very low.

"We can pay the hotel for another week, but then I really do not know what we can do," said Huniady with a melancholy shake of his head. He was thinking of the expenses for their retinue of twenty people, of the doctors required for the pregnant Archduchess, of the excessive prodigality displayed on their arrival when, in only a few days, hundreds of crowns had gone on tips to the hotel's waiters and cooks despite his pleadings for economy.

Aiku had not given that problem a thought. He himself had never needed money; for years everything had been his. If he ever wanted something, he had just had to put out his hand. But the situation on the island no longer supported his certainties of the past. However he had felt some surprise that their money had so far covered everything; seemingly that small sum had been doubled, as if by magic, over and over again along their way. He also had noticed the waiters' faces on the first evening of their exile, amazed at receiving a small fortune as a tip.

Help came from one of those sharper swings of the scales whose process of settling down represented the passage of time. A visit was one day announced from their Imperial Majesties the Emperor and Empress of Mexico, Maximilian I and Carlotta, travelling on the *Novara* towards their new empire. Marie Christine welcomed them on the hotel's finest terrace, the one overlooking the sea on three sides and, behind, at the end of a tongue of land joining the cape to the island, the central range of mountains. Aiku kept silent during the conversation, leaving it all to his wife. There in front of that ocean, immense as the great unknown accompanying the adventure of her ancestor Maximilian, the young Archduchess of Hapsburg had managed to find suitable words for Carlotta's ambitions for power and for Maximilian's lazy idealism. They were pathetic, those two, suddenly making their appearance out of a delay in history, from a backward-breaking wave caused by some distant movement, emerging from a fold in the terrific state of disorder that had catapulted the old into the new.

Marie Christine took several glasses of Madeira to overcome her compassion and embarrassment at talking with someone about whose fate she was already so well aware, but to whom she could offer no help. Could she have always seen in every human what she found in that woman, her feelings could only have been of love. Even in such a brief encounter, the present of a life yet to be lived meeting the present of another already ended, broke down any barrier between them. Carlotta never knew why she was so touched on seeing the clearly pregnant condition of the young Hapsburg; she certainly could not help seeing Maximilian's amazed expression when she insisted on donating a sum of money to cover the main necessities of childbirth on that barren island, so different from those on which the Imperial family had been accustomed to stay during their trips down the Dalmatian coast. She had realised the practical and financial difficulties besetting the couple on the island and, in the tenderness of that moment, was overcome by the wish to confide her worries over their ambitious scheme, apprehension for her adored but absent-minded husband so lacking in vitality. The man seated by her relative, so silent and severe, the Asian who made rooms seem smaller when he entered, appeared to her so strong and attractive, so sure, so protective. . .

"And then, dear, who knows if we shall ever be able to return. That sea is so immense," the Empress of Mexico suddenly sighed, watching the waves with a faraway expression, loosening the ribbons of her cap, allowing the breeze to ruffle her hair. Aiku did not know those two from past history but, at her remark, he recalled the tragic couple

130

whom Marie Christine had referred to as being a sad omen just when they were leaving Istria. He gave a start as it all suddenly became clear to him: those two were dead.

Yet that visit had brought them the money that was to last them for years, during a time of careful saving when they had to make more and more economies as the family grew. First came Elizabeth, then Otto, Madi, Yasugai, Felix, Charles Louis, Tamugin and Toregene. After the visit from the Emperor of Mexico and his wife, they decided to find somewhere less expensive to live than the luxury hotel, and accepted the offer from an importer of coffee of free accommodation. Several times he had requested the honour of housing the great general whose exile conferred distinction not only upon that lonely island, but on the entire ocean whose waves washed its shores. Up there on top of the mountain where Mr. Denys's house stood, it almost seemed a different island. The woods, the pure air and silence, the wide valleys surrounding the house helped to immerse its inhabitants in an atmosphere even more charmed and secluded. All their children naturally enjoyed to the full their freedom and close contact with nature. As the seasons changed and reappeared, as the stars made their rounds and resumed their former positions in the sky, it nevertheless became more and more difficult to remind the children, born as they had been on the island far from Vienna and Europe, of the principles of an education that could not but appear to them abstract and rather absurd. In the girls their father's wild nature seemed to prevail over the polished manners of their mother's country. As if to even matters up, the boys showed constant interest in the customs and habits taught them by their mother and never tired of listening when she told them stories about life in Vienna, of her father's exploits, and of the prestige enjoyed by their family. The one most like her

131

father, the most independent in character, was Elizabeth or Lilith as they called her at home.

One day in July Elizabeth left the house alone in search of a spring she remembererd having been taken to by the Countess Huniady. The exceptionally clear water had greatly impressed her, as had the calm of that deep pool in which she had seen not only her own reflection but also flights of birds, clouds and nearby mountain peaks. She was not quite sure of finding it again but wanted to try. She had no fear, being the eldest of the children to whom, she had often been told, she must set a good example. She thought the spring lay in the direction of the highest mountain and so took that way. Along her path it seemed that someone called her name, first near a great oak, then from the edge of a clearing where the wood was thickest. But it did not alarm her, she felt sure she had mistaken the sounds of the forest for voices. She recognised the path she had trodden two years before with Countess Huniady and thought it could not be much farther to the spring, even if that time horrid Huniady had made her walk faster. Her shoes began to hurt her and she took them off with a great feeling of relief; she had never walked barefoot so much before and found a new pleasure in it. What an adventure on a day like today. . .

She almost wished it would never end. Why fear being alone; who could harm her there? Reaching the top of a hill from where she could see over a good deal of the island, she spied Mr. Denys's villa showing palely through the trees some distance away. The second floor windows were clearly visible, one of them belonging to the room where she slept with her sisters. So that was the house where she always lived. But who was it stopped on this hill, where she now stood? Who watched her unobserved from that spot? Although, walking along, she had sensed that someone was calling her, now she felt certain of being watched by staring eyes that kept her in sight at every movement she made, eyes that had been following her in all she did long before this moment, perhaps every day, perhaps always, even while she slept, worked and talked with her sisters in that house over there now appearing so small. Elizabeth felt that someone was waiting for her among the foliage of the nearest trees, there right among the lowest branches where the path led down to the spring whose murmuring sound reached her ears, someone incapable of harming her, mild, entirely unoffending. Her desire to call out to it, give it a name, hear its voice, was stronger than her fear, and she was about to do so when at last she heard her name repeated not by one but by many mouths. Animals of all kinds appeared from the higher and lower branches, from the foliage, the grass, nearby bushes, from the path she had followed, from holes in the ground, from nests: rabbits, colts, butterflies, snakes, mice, tortoises, parrots, humming birds and many other brightly coloured species, including some that were ugly and ungainly, and who dragged their hapless forms over the ground. Elizabeth had to sit down and wait while they all found a place in the clearing, and then turn her head in an effort to hear them all one at a time, reassuring them by gestures that she would not go away because she had plenty of time and would stay till the very last – the snake – had spoken.

What the animals wished to tell her was the story of the world at its beginnings, of that garden which had welcomed man as its guest and lord, but later had had to suffer his tyrannical wickedness and violence in infinite forms. They spoke of the torment of extinct species, of the tears shed by small, almost invisible, animals and by the largest most majestic ones, all equally victims of a human order. They told these things to her, the child of him who had broken the chains of time because, with her, the world would regain its original innocence, an innocence destroyed by the male power of the descendants of Adam; they told them to her, a woman and a queen, to whom would be unveiled the mystery of that return to the past, that salvation seemingly the anxious desire of all the world, the desire of centuries. The nearest implored her to look straight at them, not to fear to love the form they wore, to observe, observe in all its implications the backward course of time, from human shape – her own – to animal form. Could she not at last see who they were? They urged that hers should not be the error committed by Eve, unable to redeem the serpent, lacking any love for him. . .

And the daughter of Aiku, grandchild of a woman who knew she must die in giving birth to an unparalleled line of descendants, felt the barrier dissolve between the visible and the invisible, between human and divine, time and the eternal. In a flash she realised what had been the divine toil, the penalty paid by him who, impelled by generosity and in a moment of tedium, had run the risk of being twice unrecognised – by nature and by history. She felt the limits imposed by shape drop away to nothingness, dissolution of the masks the Divinity was bound to assume, in the most diverse forms of life, in order to be loved; she heard him weep in the snake, lament his solitude in the toad as it jumped up into her lap.

That evening, after many hours spent in anxious search, Aiku and the servants found her lying in a faint in the clearing where close by could be heard the murmur of a spring. The grass around her, already damp with dew, appeared only lightly trodden. A long blue feather lay on the ground. What could have frightened his Lilith, wondered Aiku, as he carried her home? And while, in his arms, she slowly opened her eyes, the animals on the island told one another of a pact made with their Queen, so that the fish in the ocean and the birds flying towards distant lands should also know it. No longer would they be dominated by man; soon, very soon, death, the last of time's creatures, would be destroyed.

=== 13 ===

ONE MORNING in August 1682 the British ship reached the Atlantic island after a most trying voyage. She still bore signs of the storm which had driven her off course northward towards Portugal, a long way from the route for St. Helena. From the decks seamen in their black and white uniforms could be seen repairing the plating, mending rope ladders, replacing cables, knocking nails back into the boards, caulking the lifeboats. All the bustle appeared to be preventing passengers, whose origins no one knew, from leaving the ship. One of them certainly seemed concerned. Absorbed in thought, he stopped to light his pipe, then pointed out to his companion some features of the island, its peaks and the plume of smoke from its volcano. The two could then be seen leaning on their tools, gazing ahead, the sight of the island apparently making them more uneasy the longer they looked at it. The First Mate immediately sent an order to resume work if they wanted to sleep that night. Clearly the extent of repairs necessary would take them till dusk. Perhaps when night fell and there was nothing further to see, the Captain would be able to prepare the crew for a quick departure and the comet they had been following for three thousand leagues would reappear in the sky. Only the Captain, the English astronomer Edmund Halley, on a mission for making observations in the southern sky, had decided to leave the ship about mid-day accompanied by the Second Mate, having just learned from the Port Authorities that they were expected.

The Governor had come out on the quay to meet them. "At last the messengers have arrived! We have been waiting for you so long. Our look-outs sighted you some days ago. . ."

The newcomers introduced themselves but the Governor seemed uninterested in names and credentials, his feelings concentrated in his gaze. He observed the officers' silver-frogged uniforms as if he would devour them with his eyes; a slight tremor of emotion passed through him, and he was barely able to refrain from touching the men standing before him.

"Since no one has landed at this port for three hundred years, you will understand our excitement. As you see, the town cannot contain its joy! The last ship came in far too long ago. . ."

Such a crowd of people in fact had collected that some were in danger of falling off the quay into the water. They also expressed their feelings with looks. They said little, merely pointing out the new arrivals to each other and repeating two words: "the messengers, the messengers. . ." but spoke in so low a tone as to be unheard by the Captain and his officer, by now somewhat bemused at the Governor's words of welcome.

The English spoken by the islanders, including that of the Governor, seemed syncopated and distorted, as if reduced to a more rapid and pithy form of communication, and was initially difficult to understand; to Halley his own language seemed slow and antiquated. They, the messengers, had absolutely nothing to announce; they were there by mistake.

137

"You will have brought orders for us, for the High Protector. A great date will at last be entered in your ship's journal since you must have had a lot of trouble finding us!" came the Governor's happy and incredible words.

Messengers of what? From whom? These people were insane. With difficulty the Captain managed to shoulder his way among the throng crowding the quayside and the square in front of the Harbour Master's office.

"What a long time you took to get here!"

"What orders have you brought? Are you going to free him? Take him back with you?"

"What will become of us now if they take him away?"

"Better like that, I'd say, better if 'he' goes and his court with him."

"He's the devil, you know, the devil himself. . . You will find that out for yourselves aboard ship, the things he gets up to!" The Captain instinctively raised his hands to cover his ears to avoid hearing any more, regardless of what the Governor would think of so discourteous a gesture. He felt a strong desire to have nothing to do with these people and tried to gauge how many more steps he must still take to reach the door of the building towards which they were going and where, presumably, the crowd would not be allowed in. Thirty, perhaps forty steps, another ten minutes of that crush but more like eternity in that pose and in his state of anxiety. However, stopping his ears for those ten minutes, shutting himself off from everything, would perhaps be the saving of his identity, and mean that he and his men could still retain what seemed denied to those people – a future intact, invisible and attractive, far from any gaze, any kind of a future no matter what.

Now he could only see them, those faces, gesticulating hands, weaving bodies, without having to hear them: sirens, like those met by Ulysses, would be unable to break up his ship on the rocks. Observing them he was struck by their cheekbones, chins, the tips of their noses, rounded like none he had ever seen in any other race encountered in his voyages all over the world. A light stroke of the brush, a rub-over with pumice stone shading the outlines of their faces, smoothing off edges, softening the features, giving them all a similar expression, as if a painter had portrayed them so often that they had become worn down by his art of reproduction. To how many lost navigators had they lied as they had done to him? Their faces seemed to him so well known as to be unable to suggest anything new, as if millions of history students had contemplated them in illustrated paragraphs about the most important events of the time. Those faces were tired of being seen. They were the faces of the Dead.

He finally arrived at the Harbour Master's building as if entering a haven after a storm much more perilous than the one which had so violently shaken his ship that night. He felt saved. His Second Mate had also shut his ears. The conversation which followed did nothing to lessen his determination to leave after dark – if anything it was strengthened. The awful nature of those statements – the island was garrisoned by a regiment of soldiers, it being the seat of the High Protector, the invincible warrior who had lost contact with his own empire – somehow or other had the effect of making him feel cheerful. He pretended to co-operate as one who, having understood the various aspects of sickness, could behave like a wise doctor giving encouragement to a patient ill beyond hope. He was helpful, promised everything, adopted a winning manner, gave all the assurances they asked for, and stated that he would be available first thing the next morning once repairs to the ship had been completed. It would indeed be an honour to sail away with the High Protector on board; this in fact was the essence of his instructions; even if he had never read the messages themselves, that was the purpose of their mission. The mate, who had kept quiet throughout, confirmed his Captain's words with nods.

Now had come the moment for leave-taking; most of the crowd had dispersed, there was no longer any noise round the building. When saying goodbye to each other, the two commanders – of the island and of the ship – knew with perfect clarity the truth about the lies each had told the other. Both knew that neither could free the other from his destiny, already decided for the Governor, though still uncertain and obscure for the English astronomer. Overcome by a strange emotion, the sides became reversed: the dead Governor was seized by a longing to recreate his personality, to abandon the perfection of Death; while the living astronomer felt drawn towards the irresponsibility of perpetually awaiting the dead who came to be shattered on the shores of that island, breaking like the long wave of a calm sea. Amazed, the Second Mate heard his Captain say:

"Do not envy me, we are condemned to be free, we know nothing of our future."

When early next day the Governor and his staff went down to the quay where Halley's ship had berthed, he made no comment on finding nothing there. He picked up a piece of frayed rope hanging down over the water and studied the horizon, empty as usual, a clean line as if cut with a knife.

Far out to sea, all sight of the island having disappeared as from a dream, the young astronomer stood next to the helmsman checking their route towards the Equator, heading for St. Helena guided by the comet once more visible on that clear night, distinct and pulsating, with a tail so bright and so long that it stretched across the greater part of the sky. When, penetrating low-lying cloud one morning, Halley saw through his telescope the sharp outline of Diana's Peak, the highest mountain on St. Helena, he at last opened his journal and noted the date of that memorable day.

He began then to believe that the comet had called him to be present at the ending of the world, had begun to show him that the confines of time were those of a condemned empire. That island they had just left, unmarked on any map yet caught in the incubus of a tragic myth, and this one, marked on all maps yet of slight significance, possessing no legend whereby it could be otherwise described than 'St. Helena, a small island'. . . For the first time he understood that not by scientific passion had he been moved to leave England for the ocean in search of that star. His constitutional disbelief in there being any chance of changing the course of events, of effectively expressing his opposition to corrupt government as exercised by Charles II and his clique at court, his melancholy recollections of adolescence overshadowed by an austere father (an old companion in arms of Cromwell, who bitterly hated the restored dynasty), all suddenly found cohesion in his hidden hope of a catastrophe. He wanted the end of the world, did Halley, incapable of controlling his own destiny but also unwilling to accept what might come. The comet was this: the sign of a hoped-for rebirth, nurtured for so long like an inadmissible desire in face of all that was most distasteful to him in his times and in his country, but which he felt he could not even partially correct or heal. Such was the cold reasoning which caused him to believe that this comet was the same one that had appeared in the sky to remind men of their fate as creatures condemned without hope of reprieve. Applying the theory of universal gravitation recently elaborated by his compatriot Isaac Newton, in the long nights of study he had passed on St. Helena in the summer of 1682, wandering over those inaccessible mountains, seemingly created purposely to form a background for solitary explorations of a truth, he had deduced that, since the orbits of 1607 and 1531 were practically identical, it must be the same comet moving round the sun. And, having proved its elliptical orbit meant that the comet could be seen from the earth at intervals of seventy-five years – the average span of human life – he moved on from one calculation to another, reconstructing over past ages the times of its many appearances, until some indefinable moment one night when it was sighted for the first time.

Halley was never able to fix the date. Not because of fatigue or mathematical complexities; none of that. A lady cat intervened to dissuade him from marking that most distant point of consciousness, that limit to knowledge evoking a world only just emerging from the mists of prehistory – producing its first plants, its first animals, and earliest man. The cat, appearing from some farm buildings near the bottom of the hill, continued the plaintive miaowing which obliged him to abandon his train of thought and attend to her. He soon realised that her call was an appeal for help; clearly she was in the throes of giving birth. Her large green eyes held his, imploring aid, and he felt unable to deny her plea. Recalling his childhood and his nurse helping their cat at Haggerson in similar circumstances, he forgot he was there, on St. Helena, to observe the comet; and massaging and stroking her to assist her contractions, he remained beside her all night. The sheltering tree above them seemed desirous of guarding the birth of the kittens from the indiscreet gaze of the stars, as if some sacred property protected any event under its foliage. By dawn the cat, tortoise-shell with white markings, had given birth to eight kittens: four white, two orange, two like their mother. Touched by this appealing sight, it seemed to Halley that life was calling on him to respect its mysteries, as if some force higher than his thirst for knowledge and his catastrophic pessimism were dissuading him from going beyond a certain limit. The kittens were already sucking their mother's milk. New life had entered the cycle. To no one was it granted to determine the end and the beginning of time.

14

THAT VAST drifting movement bringing centuries into collision, like islands which float without foundations, causing encounters and confusion among the powerful and the popes, among revolutions, political regimes and armed forces, confusing titles, prerogatives and functions – all this occurred almost entirely in what was called the Old World, in the three continents of Europe, Asia and Africa which perhaps in prehistoric times had never really been divided. Only America and Japan remained moving along the rails of their age, as if the series of events that had brought the terrible power of the Tartar leader on the scene no longer concerned them. World equilibrium, already so precarious, could hardly fail to feel the sudden lack of so many peoples even in those two countries, true though it was that billions of other men in the two nations spared by the '1815 syndrome' were being born, and living and dying with almost greater impetus than before, filling a gap and carrying out duties suddenly neglected in the shortage of human beings.

Children seemed the most sensitive instruments for measuring the state of deterioration suffered by the great mass of the earth: in the United States, through their play, they soon exorcised that vague fear of disappearing into nothing instilled into them by their parents' silence on the subject. As if by magic a game of hide-and-seek of nations spread through nurseries and primary schools. In one class the children acted being a European, Asian or African country, each with a differently coloured skin, wearing a certain type of headgear, dressed in a certain way. When one child had hidden, another classmate had to guess which country was missing.

So, through play, some rudimentary knowledge of the whole planet was saved; famous traditions, notions and customs were recalled to mind as, when learning about the Phoenicians and Carthaginians, these same children read about purple being extracted from certain seashells, or learned that, at Carthage, Hannibal's warring tendencies were opposed by the peaceful forces of Hanno. Who among them had ever seen the purple-giving seashell? What interest could they feel in the forces for war or peace in Carthage? Yet no one had ever protested at having to learn about such far-off days. Thus Italy had become a game of surprises, at one time appearing as a dark-haired little girl holding a tambourine for dancing the tarantella, singing and throwing kisses at the others while, at other times, there were more sophisticated and mischievous disguises when, among the bigger pupils, that country was represented by a boy wearing a white cassock and tall tubular hat, hands raised in the act of blessing; partly pagan and partly Christian.

Better certainly than in other cases. Russia, for instance, was always dressed up as a brown bear, awakening in the children old hatreds and long-standing rivalry with the derelict Slav nation who had paid the highest price in her defence to the last against the monster from Mongolia. France was usually portrayed as a heavily made-up little girl with such daring lipstick and highly back-combed hair, in such exceedingly high-heeled shoes as to leave no doubt about the disguise being that of a street-walker.

Invention found greatest fulfilment in the East; where Asia was concerned there was no limit to the children's fantasies. No rules were set for disguises and these were constantly varied. Each time something new was devised, always in very bright colours. Though countries in Asia, and some of the oldest in Africa, were the most amusing to imagine, giving scope for remote associations of the unconscious mind, they were also the hardest to guess because of their ambiguity. There was little demand for them in the games of children accustomed to binary logic. Teachers, irritated and slightly scornful, complained that in the East, apart from Japan, computer-based reasoning did not function – as if explaining to themselves that Aiku's birth had taken place there, and that it was not by chance the continent was incapable of adapting to the spirit of the times. And in so much foolishness, in the confused minds of those who admit something is equal to itself and to its opposite, many Americans found an explanation for the inferiority of those exterminated peoples, an explanation current not only in the hide-and-seek at schools, but also in Congress and at the White House.

Edmund Halley, the American Secretary of State, had become convinced that binary logic would be useful to the President to save his conscience in the face of the horrifying and inexplicable disappearance into nothing of so many lives; as if the physical destruction of all those nations could be the result of a kind of guilt, an indirect responsibility of the peoples concerned. Those who survive deserve to do so, the President appeared to think, though he never dared say it openly. When, for some reason, and after several months of increasingly apparent conflict, Halley gave in his resignation, it seemed to the President quite logical and necessary; nor did he ask himself whether it might not be useful to have a dialectically-minded and critical interlocutor like Halley beside him for governing in a situation so abnormal and so unlike anything the country had gone through in the whole of its history – a situation requiring imagination and spirit of adventure rather than consolidated methods and tradition.

The evening after his resignation Halley, who was un-married and lived partly with his father John, the Presbyterian pastor, at his farm about sixty miles distant, was on his way to Washington driving himself in his Saab. He thought over the last conversation at the White House, marked by underlying hostility, when he had taken his letter of resignation to the President; he recalled the false and unctuous ceremonial of welcome, the words expressing formal regret and thanks, the question about his future plans. Everything had been conducted according to the worn-out formula of pensioning off an enemy; only one remark had stung the suavely impassive President when Halley had replied to his question about what he meant to do now that he was free of Government engagements.

"I am going to study history, Mr. President. We Americans do not have a very long one, neither do we understand those whose history is ancient and who carry it within them like a disease. You could have been an excellent doctor for this malady; together we could have done something to help the Europeans recover."

"What an imagination you have, my dear Halley! Rather *too* much perhaps for an American Secretary of State?"

"Yes, Mr. President, you're right."

"In any case, from today on I shall regretfully have to do without it," had come the other's chilly rejoinder.

147

And they had taken leave of each other then, without saying anything about meeting again in some other place. Two who said goodbye in that way should never see each other again alive, thought Halley, as he overtook a coach on the highway. A short way farther on a luminous sign appeared on the right limiting the road to a single lane and warning there would be a detour within two miles because of a landslide. The traffic had slowed down but not sufficiently to take Halley's mind off his thoughts which still revolved around the President and that last talk at the White House. Who would come to take his place? Wolff perhaps, a luke-warm dull personality, or perhaps Newman. No; more likely they would choose Frost, since no one was better able to echo the President than he, who had run the Bank of America for so many years and saw reality only as a world of opposing financial interests and of capital to invest somewhere or other.

Preoccupied with unhappy thoughts about his exit from the scene, Halley suddenly became aware that the detour off the highway was about to begin, brought to his notice by the black figures of police standing to wave on traffic and keep it moving. He could see traces of a recent landslide caused by the heavy rain there had been for the past two days. Mud had spread over the asphalt, a few holes in the surface shook the car. After a mile or so, instead of signs to lead drivers back onto the main route, the road seemed to Halley darker and more lonely than usual as if it never had been a temporary diversion from the highway but always an out-of-the-way and little used road. Cars passed less frequently, oncoming ones became fewer and fewer but, as time went by, these too disappeared and no others passed him. He could see no lights nor road signs, no indication of built-up areas, no mentions of distances or place names; nothing. Only the headlamps of his blue Saab pierced the dark, two ribbons of light on the smooth black asphalt, perfect with no holes. Too perfect for this kind of secondary road. Halley's mind no longer held any image of the President or of the White House. The past had gone, replaced by a strange scenario of the present, emptier than in any dream, blacker, more unnerving.

He realised that he was lost, that he – always so proud of his sense of direction, one who boasted he could find his way in any city he visited for the first time – had missed (but when?) the point at which he should have rejoined the main highway, and was now on some other leading he knew not where. There was nothing to be done except to continue till he reached some place, hoping his fuel would last out – the tank was half-full – and that he could finish that journey; but when would it end? Meeting no other vehicles, people, houses or signposts, with just the light emitted by his car, and therefore unreal since it came not from outside but was only willed by him, Halley went on driving, bent over the wheel as if wanting to convey to the vehicle all his firm intention of getting somewhere. Two hours passed in this way. His forehead damp with sweat and with a feeling of nausea coming over him, perhaps because he had not eaten for so long, the ex-Secretary of State was becoming aware how risky was this absurd situation, his fuel indicator now showing danger level. Another thirty-five miles or so and the car would stop. Where? He had no idea at all where he was.

Looking to one side and the other and to the dark night behind him, in no direction was there any sign of dawn. It must be after four: he glanced at the clock on the dashboard; it said midnight. He checked his watch. That had stopped too, but at eleven. How strange they had both stopped. Inwardly he felt certain what the time was, the only certainty

allowing him to hope for the light of dawn when at last he
would be able to see his surroundings. The sun at any rate
would have to rise, it could hardly fail to. And yet, thinking
over his journey, nothing had been certain. In such a desolate
spot it might be that the sun would not rise, as if it could only
derive from the living the strength to rise each morning. But
he felt alive and he wanted the sun as much as a million
people all put together. He touched his body to make sure
it was alive and that he could continue to occupy space and
volume. Without knowing it he was repeating the gesture of
primitive man who feared he would die on the first evening
he saw the sun setting and night approaching.

Just then he felt he could go no further, and drew up,
leaving the lights on. He opened the door and got out,
taking a deep breath as if in danger of suffocating. Wiping
the perspiration from his brow, he unbuttoned his trousers
and urinated. That give him an indefinable sense of relief
and relaxation and he closed his eyes as the smell of the urine
rose in the damp air. His body was alive, that seemed proved
beyond doubt. Again he looked in front of him, behind and
above, but could see neither stars, hills nor trees. There was
a dark mist everywhere; only in the beams of his headlamps
did it seem milky and more diaphanous. What was it best
to do? He was too short of fuel to think of going back;
all he could do was to continue, in the hope of reaching
some inhabited place. Backward or forward might no longer
have any significance since space seemed now to have no
direction, time having none after his watch had stopped.
Half an hour or so later the car also stopped. He left it where
it was and began to walk along the right hand verge of the
road guided for a few hundred yards by its headlights. When
they too went out, perhaps because the battery had failed,
his heart seemed to miss a beat; he could go no further in

the dark and fog, that was no way for the living. But having abandoned his car, its lights, his watch, and the highway, having left the world in which he had lived for forty-nine years, just then the first rays of dawn began to show. The fog lifted and outlines of a mountainous landscape could be faintly discerned, one that he failed to recognise. A short while later higher crests came into view, ranges of bare rocky peaks, steep and tall, a sinister disconsolate scene. But the sun was up though veiled by cloud through which penetrated a cold and pearly light.

He reached the river where he found a crowd of people assembled, people like himself who had left their road and lost their way – the favoured ones who, in their hearts, had some time ago resigned their posts, their tasks, their faith, their roles and, like automata, lived with their bodies only, lacking any prescience of the birth and truth of a new world.

It all happened with great simplicity. On the river bank he met his namesake and ancestor who, one night on St. Helena, had neglected his studies of the comet to help a cat give birth to her kittens, Edmund Halley the English astronomer. He too had manifested the same rejection of his times as his descendant was to do later; perhaps it was the fate of their family. Possessed by a dream of newborn humanity, he too had sought in the skies, in his long exploration of the solitary untroubled pathways of the stars, a diversion, a gateway, a proof that all must be destroyed to be rebuilt. He had believed in that comet, among twenty-four he had observed, that comet which, according to his calculations had left its orbit and was destined to crash onto the earth; he had allowed himself to think that, in departing from its path, it would set man on a fresh course in the world, one in which no evil, no imperfection – such as at present existed – would find their place.

151

Waiting for the ferry boat for the crossing, the two Halleys discussed this very point as if they had always known one another.

"My mistake," said the astronomer, "was made in thinking there was a single world to destroy so that a new one could be created. There are many of them; God, it seems, became tired of being alone and amused Himself by making a great quantity. At the most my comet could destroy only one, and so would preserve all the others. Evil would therefore continue in other worlds since none ever left its Creator's hands perfect."

"But your comet did not even hit the earth."

"It did, however, make a disaster certain. I wanted that much. You cannot really believe it is sufficient to destroy matter. . . Much more effective was terror or faith, or whatever you would call it. You, for that matter, merely lost your way – though in actual fact you no longer wanted to return and so gave in your resignation."

"And all these people?"

"Like yourself they are tired. By this I mean they have found the energy to live in some other place. Like us they are waiting to move into another world, not to 'the other', as the over-simplified expression has it. And each person will go to the world he most of all missed in the one he inhabited. The lack of, and wish for, the world he most needed have together become the force able to evoke the new one."

"But what has atomic imbalance to do with all this?"

"It speeded up the whole process by which each one identifies with his double celestial sphere. The ache had become too great, neuroses tormented more than half the living, and the explosion was inevitable. You perceived this in some obscure way, like some others, and you were thus ripe for leaving your road, for crossing over to the other bank."

More travellers arrived just then, they too perfectly calm and controlled, and each found someone they recognised and could converse with as the two Halleys had done.

The descendant felt no curiosity to ask his ancestor from where he had come to give him a welcome. Clearer than ever came the awareness, now usual to him, that the world of each was incommunicable. The astronomer's words surprised him; they sounded as if he were thinking aloud rather than talking to him. "Those sovereigns at Vienna did not hate Aiku enough; they did not realise that their salvation, and that of everyone, would come from a hate for him which he himself urged them to feel. They did not understand the role of evil and so they could not enact the role of good. Now everything must be done all over again, trusting men will be more intelligent this time, more imaginative than before."

"Do you want me to believe that the same chain of events can be repeated?"

"Not once but a hundred, a thousand times, till it comes out perfect: the battle of Waterloo, the Congress of Vienna have been repeated seven times and, as you see, must continue to be repeated. It is hard to distinguish the subtleties between one attempt and another but not impossible – as among various executions of a symphony. For that matter, everything is a duplicate but is even so itself; myself in relation to you. I preceded you in name and surname, Edmund Halley, in the hope of an end, in the weariness of the old world, because I was saturated with myself and with my egoism, with my race, a master race yet stupid in its superiority, but am I not different from you? To reach my perfection I too have had to beget a son who begot another, and so on down to you, who will not beget any since you are the most complete of all of us. Some great men too, if you only knew how many times they have had to beget

153

facsimiles of themselves before achieving their model! Now listen carefully to this: that very Aiku was preceded by at least another six like himself but, as you have seen, he was unable to. . ."

He could not finish his sentence because the boat arrived from the opposite bank. Ancestor and desendant took leave of each other with a smile. The ex-Secretary of State of that power which had been the counterweight and mirror of Aiku's empire, embarked. Soon after, he saw the astronomer move away and disappear. He turned. The opposite shore could just be seen. He knew that a village of Mongolian shepherds awaited him, a blind grandfather, a beautiful mother from an island in the Japanese archipelago, the city of Urga, his name which, in his mother's tongue, signified 'man', an army blindly faithful to him, an army that would follow him to a new conquest of the world.